LEGEND OF LOVADA BRANCH

BOOK ONE: THE COVE

LEGEND OF LOVADA BRANCH

BOOK ONE: THE COVE

To Nancy – with grateful prayer! Karen & Paul

Karen Karper Fredette

Illustrated by Paul A. Fredette

iv

*Lovingly dedicated to
our mother in courage and in life,
Georgette Lucille Arbour-Fredette*

Acknowledgments

A work of fiction that has been many years in formation owes its life and final form to many events - folks, near and far whose lives have intersected mine, often unknowingly, as well as to the inherent evolution of the writer wrought by Life.

My special gratitude flows out to a unique people who have preserved their heritage and culture for centuries in the ancient mountains of western North Carolina. Their music, their language, their particular outlook on life provided me, as a writer, with the necessary context in which to set my particular inspiration.

I am indebted to Charles Williams for his notion of effective prayer, depicted in "War in Heaven" and found here on pg. 90 and to T. S. Eliot for the final stanza of his poem, "Ash Wednesday", quoted on pp. 195-196.

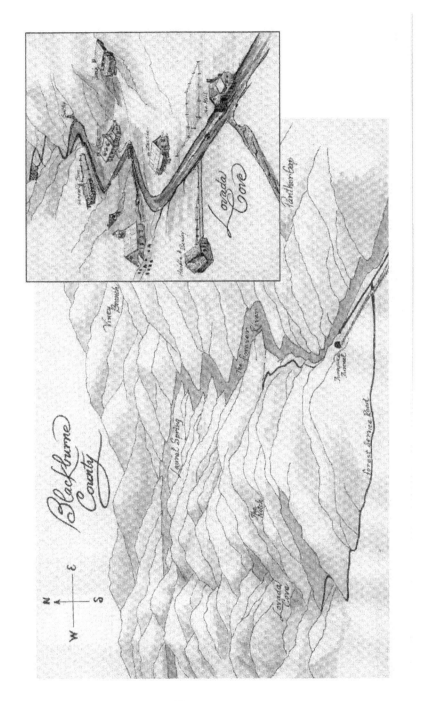

viii

CHAPTER ONE

The silence before the scream arrested Kyle in mid-step. Apprehension sandpapered his every nerve and skittered like cat claws up his back. Captive in that soundless instant, as if before a cracking tree falls, Kyle waited, uncertain where to leap.

"Eiyow!" A piercing shriek confirmed the prescience that was his curse and his gift. Swinging around, Kyle saw his wife, Wren, thrashing wildly in the shallow ford he had just crossed, beating the rock-strewn water of Loverly Creek with her hiking staff. "Snake, snake," she screeched as she struggled for footing. Hampered by the pack on his back, Kyle sprang toward her, grabbing for her flailing arms.

Blinded by her terror, Wren missed his grasp and crashed heavily to her knees in the muddied waters. Snagging one of Wren's shoulder straps, Kyle managed to heave his struggling wife up and onto the bank. Wren swayed, dripping and panting, her eyes wildly scanning the tangled growth surrounding them. Copperheads and rattlesnakes were said to be rampant along this branch of the Forever River that tumbled down a southern slope of Unaka Mountain. Carefully, Kyle guided Wren toward a low boulder beside

1

the trail, where she collapsed, letting her pack slide from her trembling shoulders. Dilated pupils masked her normally blue-green eyes, blurring her manic search of the May greenery about them. Wrapping his arms around Wren, Kyle rocked her, stroking her short reddish hair as shudders coursed through her slight frame. When Wren's eyes finally refocused, she smiled wanly up at Kyle who was regarding her with a mixture of concern and surprise. His normally feisty woman cuddled against him, eliciting the protective instincts in him that she ordinarily rejected. Kyle's brow creased in confusion over this prickly, independent lady who occasionally dissolved in terror, overcome by phobic fears. His long brown fingers gently kneaded Wren's shoulders, expressing the surge of love her vulnerability evoked in him.

Sighing, Wren snuggled more deeply into Kyle's embrace, savoring being cradled in strong, warm arms in her moment of panic. Such comfort was a dizzying gift she had felt compelled to test over and over during the three years of their marriage. But as Kyle had made it abundantly clear that she was the major focus of his life, Wren's many anxieties had begun to diminish. This hike into the Smokey Mountain wilderness was one expression of her growing trust.

Easing his own pack onto the mossy ground, Kyle settled back against a thick poplar and pulled Wren against his chest. Her rapid breathing evened out as she slowly relaxed against him. Eliciting Wren's trust reminded Kyle of the time he had tamed an abandoned fox kit - a long and ticklish affair.

Half-reclining on the leaf-strewn ground, Kyle and Wren listened to the finches and nuthatches chattering overhead, their chirps and whistles mingling with the gurgle of Loverly Creek. Stirring finally, her plaintive whisper barely audible amid the forest voices, Wren murmured, "Why is it they scare me so? I just panicked when I saw that wavy shadow in the water."

Kyle nodded and chaffed her cold hands between his own larger ones. Snakes figured largely in Wren's repertoire of phobias. Even this terror, however, had not prevented her planning this backpacking trek with him into a seldom traversed section of the Smokies. Kyle, tanned and sturdy, was as at home in the woods as his Cherokee ancestors. His dark brown eyes surveyed their path instinctively and he would have noticed a snake near the ford. Other instincts, however, told him this was no time to suggest that Wren rein in her imagination. Instead he complimented Wren on her alertness and smoothed her disheveled hair.

Wren gazed up into Kyle's broad-featured face, her fingers tracing his prominent cheekbones and square jaw line lovingly. When a smile quirked the corners of his often grim lips, she touched them gently, wonderingly. Kissing her teasing fingers, Kyle shifted her small frame more securely onto his knees.

A busy gray squirrel, scurrying overhead, dislodged some petals that sifted down into Wren's lap. Tucking his silvering hair more securely under his headband, Kyle glanced upward. A Great Laurel, rooted in an overhanging rock, drooped over them. When Kyle offered Wren a fragile blossom, she drew a deep breath and smiled.

"Remember?" she whispered, and Kyle nodded, his smile moving up into his eyes. "Only three years ago," she marveled, rubbing their rings together.

"You were worth waiting for," he declared quietly, seeing amused gratitude chasing itself across Wren's mobile features.

"You finally rescued this old maid," she giggled, wondering fleetingly how it was that Kyle, too, had entered a first marriage only in his early thirties. The work of melding their diverse careers and interests had pushed a number of unasked questions about Kyle's past onto a back burner in

Wren's mind. But observing him function so comfortably on the trail today was arousing her suppressed curiosity.

This backpacking trip was their deferred honeymoon. Much of their camping gear was borrowed but the goal of this hike was uniquely their own. Pursuing her hobby of researching the history of western North Carolina, Wren was focusing on Blackburne County when she stumbled across the place-name, "Lovada Cove", in an old text about the short-lived State of Franklin. Typical of mountain folk, a section of what is now eastern Tennessee and northwestern North Carolina had declared itself a free and independent state in 1784. It was populated by men and women who had migrated there after the Revolutionary War and who deeply resented any attempt by outside authorities to regulate their lives.

She had also learned that Lovada Cove was located near the headwaters of Lovada Branch, a rocky stream which meandered through the Unaka Mountains along the Tennessee/North Carolina border. By comparing an old sketch with a newer map, Wren discovered that the present-day Loverly Creek, a tributary that emptied into the Forever River, was originally called Lovada Branch.

Consulting Miss Althea, Blackburne County's librarian and local historian, Wren inquired about Lovada Cove. To her surprise, Miss Althea, usually so forthcoming about local lore, only reluctantly admitted that ... "well, yes, used to be folks lived back up Lovada Cove. Some of my mother's kin come from there."

Wren studied the petite septuagenarian in her high-necked blouse and waited.

"But ... not no more," Miss Althea added with startling finality.

"No more?" Wren frowned, her surprise mingling with frustration.

"No. The only way back in there was a railroad that

washed out during a rainy spring, oh, some seventy years ago. Guess the folk just give up and left," Miss Althea surmised in her soft voice.

"Where did they all go?" Wren exclaimed.

Miss Althea pursed her lips and shifted uneasily in her chair. Clearly the topic unsettled her. Swinging back to her card file, Miss Althea looked over her shoulder at Wren, "Away, dearie, away."

When she could get no more from Miss Althea, Wren broached the topic with Kyle who inquired about Lovada Cove among the seniors at the Center where he taught manual arts. His questions evoked suspicious glances and uneasy silences. Finally, Gaither, a lean, leather-skinned mountain man, cleared his throat and spat on the ground.

"When Ah was comin' up, Ah hunted Unaka Mountain with some Cherokee buddies. 'Aire's an old rail bed runnin' 'longside of Loverly Creek that might could lead back to that cove," he drawled.

Had he been there? Gaither's eyes narrowed and he studied Kyle with brief but keen interest. "Not for you to know ... yit," he muttered and resumed his sphinxlike staring, a pipe clamped firmly between his five remaining teeth.

This growing mystery surrounding the mention of Lovada Cove troubled Kyle. Wren's middle name was Lovada, as had been her mother's and possibly her grandmother's as well. Wren had told Kyle about the Haggard family that had sheltered her unwed mother during her pregnancy. They had generously brought Wren up as one of their own brood when it became clear she was abandoned. They knew nothing about Wren's birth family. The young mother had given her name only as Della Lovada and said that she had "come up" in neighboring "Bloody Blackburne" County.

Della had disappeared a week after Wren's birth. When the child reached school-age, Wren's foster parents

5

converted her name from Winnie Lovada to the more "citified" Wren Linda. In her teens, Wren had begun asking questions about her birthmother. The hospital records listed her solely as Della Lovada of Blackburne County. But Wren's foster mother remembered Della's comment about the unusual middle name. "Lovada," Della had said, "is the only family link I can give my baby girl ... but it will be enough."

Before they were married, Wren had shown Kyle a small silver disk, crudely etched with wavy lines indicating flowing water on one side; and on the reverse, a coiled snake. Her foster mother had told her that a young man had come to their door shortly after Della's disappearance and given it to them, saying merely that Della wanted her daughter to have it. Before Glenda Haggard could ask any more questions, the man had swung off the porch and into his pick-up. Wren had worn the disk, threaded on a chain, since childhood despite her ambivalent feelings toward the mother who had abandoned her. It had become a talisman of protection against her many fears.

Those fears weren't evident when Kyle first saw Wren. In fact, he had been impressed by her poise as she addressed a conference for compensatory education teachers he was attending. Her small, neat figure and dark reddish hair contrasted sharply with the more matronly figures of most of the women present. In a field of social service dominated by women, Kyle usually huddled with the handful of men at these compulsory gatherings.

This time however, he had made it a point to strike up a conversation with Wren and discovered they shared a common passion for bettering the plight of unemployable men and women whose population was disproportionately high in the more isolated pockets of the rural mountains. Wren's job as a supervisor for Rehabilitative Education at Western Carolina University had recently expanded when

6

the state allocated more funding for off campus sites. The Center in Blackburne County where Kyle taught "city English" and manual arts became one of the sites Wren visited.

Imperceptibly, Wren found herself drawn to this gentle, dark-eyed man with the striking crop of silvery hair. Observing him "at work" on one occasion, Wren was amused as he tried to impress upon one of the mountain men the advantage of using a handkerchief. He had pulled one from his own pocket and waved it before the man's set face.

"Do you know what this is?" he had demanded.

The man retorted. "It's a snot rag. Ah may be mountain but Ah'm not stupid!"

Eventually, Wren found it necessary to visit the Blackburne County site almost weekly. The warmth of Kyle's friendship had gradually melted the professional veneer that had been her shield for years.

Raised in New England, Kyle had retained the quiet friendliness of the mountains where his family had originated. He had moved to Blackburne County a few years earlier because he said, he missed these mountains. But Wren suspected that appreciation for the scenery was not the only motive for Kyle's choice of this remote area. His Cherokee blood was obvious. This region had been and still was home to many of his people. Kyle had returned to the same Smokey Mountains that had sheltered and saved some of his ancestors from a brutal relocation order that ultimately resulted in the Trail of Tears. Was he also hiding in these hills?

The college records Wren had shamelessly plundered in order to learn more about Kyle, had revealed that his Master's degree was in theology, with undergraduate degrees in forestry and philosophy. It seemed a strange preparation for the field in which he now worked with such

7

devoted competence. Despite the mysteries that clustered about Kyle's past, or possibly because of them, Wren responded to his clear invitation and risked a closer relationship. Before long, Kyle's students began asking when the wedding bells would ring. The question had surprised both of them. Thirtyish and career-oriented, neither had seriously considered the option. Wren instinctively feared any emotional entanglement that risked rejection; Kyle carried angers and secrets he felt precluded marriage.

Their decision to marry despite these doubts and fears had proven both challenging and deeply rewarding. With only occasional rocky moments, when Wren's anxieties and Kyle's angers provoked sharp words, their mutual love had relieved much of the loneliness that had burdened both of them. Gradually, the anger which Wren had harbored toward the mother who had abandoned her diminished.

As their trust increased, Kyle evoked a vein of playfulness in Wren that she had seldom indulged even in her earliest years. For Kyle, it was like revisiting another life, at once sweet and bitter. Their mountain friends sometimes shook their heads over their "foolery" even while admitting it matched their own pleasure in joshing and play-parties.

Wren had told Kyle the meager facts she knew of her family background but he had confided little to Wren about his earlier life. Wren was content not to know. That Kyle's past might conceal conflicts and commitments that could threaten her present happiness was something Wren refused to consider. It was sufficient that he loved her now. Surprisingly, it was Kyle who had suggested that Wren read up on Blackburne County history in the hope she might discover more about her origins, never suspecting that his own history might also be laid bare.

When Wren stumbled upon a text about Lovada Cove, they both recognized it as an important breakthrough. Old

Gaither's reluctant revelation about the abandoned rail line along present-day Loverly Creek focused their interest. So when planning their delayed honeymoon, Wren and Kyle decided to search for the mysterious Lovada Cove among the lush ridges and hidden valleys of the region. What might the swirling mists of the Smokies conceal?

Now Kyle studied Wren with subdued amusement as she stripped off her wet socks and wiped out her soaked boots. Her jeans clung wetly to her slim legs, provoking pleasant movements within Kyle's visceral regions. Folding his arms across his chest Kyle intoned ponderously: "So, ho, Sloshing Bird, where do we go from here?"

Glancing up, Wren caught his scarcely veiled invitation. Flung through the air, a dripping sock caught Kyle full in the face.

"Take that, Wet Blanket!" she quipped.

"Ah, ha, the lady is thinking of blankets," Kyle crowed and made motions toward unstrapping his bedroll.

"Kyle!" Wren protested, "Not here, not now...."

"No?" responded Kyle, miming extreme disappointment while inwardly glad to see Wren had regained her spirit. "Are you ready to move on?" he asked, after Wren had fished a pair of dry socks from her pack and pulled on her boots again.

"I want to ... if I can." Wren fingered the disk that lay beneath her tee shirt and gamely struggled to her feet, testing her bruised knees. Her limp roused Kyle's concern. The path they had been following along the tumbling waters of Loverly Creek was rugged, strewn with rocks and fallen branches.

While Wren finished lacing her boots, Kyle studied the terrain about them with a woodsman's eye, finally focusing on the mountain laurel hanging above them. It sprouted from a rocky bank that appeared suspiciously man-made. Scrambling up, Kyle discovered a level cinder path edged by railroad ties. The old rail bed! The rails themselves were gone but the ties had been tossed aside and left to rot. Despite a vague unease about this unexpected discovery, Kyle knew that the cinder and gravel foundation would be far easier for Wren to manage than the uneven ground closer to the Branch.

Reaching down between the laurel branches, Kyle hoisted their packs up the bank and then gave Wren a hand up as she scrambled to join him. Limiting their hiking to easy stages, Kyle once again admired Wren's gritty determination to reach a goal she had set for herself, Wren soldiered on for several more hours before Kyle called a halt. Her gamine face was drawn with pain and weariness despite the slow pace Kyle had set.

In the course of the afternoon, Kyle's vague misgivings about this trail had concretized into definite apprehension. Even Wren had begun to notice something peculiar about this woodland path. Not only was it smoother than expected but almost no vegetation had sprung up on it. Shrubs and briars entwined thickly along the steep slopes to either side but only low grasses covered the abandoned rail bed. Kyle's hackles prickled. Neither fallen branches nor rocks littered the ground where wheel ruts were faintly visible.

The noise of rushing water had faded to a whisper as the rail bed climbed out of the gorge that Loverly Creek had carved for itself. In late afternoon, Kyle decided to pitch camp beside a small spring gushing out of the mountainside above the path. The bruises on Wren's knees were darkening to purple but the day's walking had kept her legs limber. As soon as they had slipped off their backpacks, Kyle dipped Wren's still damp socks in the cold spring water and wrapped them around her knees.

Wren smiled gratefully as the aching diminished. She began to survey their surroundings with more interest and asked Kyle about the culvert that channeled the spring water under the rail bed. Shouldn't it have become clogged over the years? She wrinkled her forehead thoughtfully, voicing Kyle's unspoken concerns. "This path looks so ... so well-kept up. If it's been seventy years since the tracks were torn up....."

"This trail should be all but gone," Kyle muttered, and began ranging about, examining the thick stands of laurel on either side of the trail. Wren silently watched him, admiring the catlike movements of this man who scanned the woods about them with a practiced eye. He looked so at home in the wild, his faded flannel shirt and jeans blending into the lengthening shadows. Yet, the further into the woods they hiked, the more of a stranger Kyle seemed to become. At times like this he reminded her of a hunted creature seeking a safe refuge from ... what? Wren shivered. A suspicion that her strong, self-reliant husband might be haunted by some unnamed grief or anger, teased and disturbed her.

Abruptly, Wren shook her head and struggled to her feet. This was not a train of thought she wanted to pursue. Kyle Makepeace had given her his name, the only name she could fully call her own. Nothing must be allowed to threaten the sense of security she had found as his wife.

Loping back to Wren, Kyle waved a branch. "Hey, look at this. I would swear that this tip here was sliced clean, not broken off. Other branches near it also look like they've been deliberately slashed back."

Kyle and Wren searched one another's faces, grappling with the same thought. It was no accident that this rail bed had remained passable all these years. Some folks were using it on a regular basis. Tales of drug trafficking across the state line suddenly acquired a sinister immediacy. "And before drugs, it probably served those who ran corn liquor," Kyle surmised. "No wonder the locals spread tales about

11

snakes and bears on Unaka Mountain."

Wren glanced about nervously as the late May evening closed in. "I hope no one plans to do business tonight," she murmured. Kyle heartily agreed. Now he regretted not heeding friends' warnings against camping without a gun. Although trained to shoot since his youth, Kyle hated the violence guns incited and refused to own one. But what if Wren were threatened?

A nearly full moon would soon rise over the eastern shoulder of the mountains, brightening the darkness so that anyone familiar with this path could walk it without the aid of a flashlight. And what four-legged creatures of the night might also avail themselves of this veritable highway through the wilderness? Kyle began to second-guess the wisdom of camping so near the path and the spring. But it was too late now to find another suitable site.

While Wren unpacked their cooking gear and supplies, Kyle gathered dry wood and kindling, taking time to scan their surroundings more closely. Reassured when he found no sign of recent passage by any other than the shyer forest beasts, Kyle returned to their campsite and soon built up a lively blaze. The warmth and light cheered Wren and she paid close heed as Kyle demonstrated how to prepare a meal on the trail. They hunkered near the fire, their arms touching frequently, arousing pleasurable promise of something more that evening.

Catching an affirmative gleam in Wren's eyes as they licked the last of their sausages from their fingers, Kyle quickly popped open their low tent. Wren rinsed their few utensils with hot water left over in the kettle and Kyle packed them up with the rest of their supplies. Deftly he strung their food bundles over a branch above easy reach of the black bears whose scat Kyle had occasionally noticed along the trail.

While Wren slithered into their tent undressing as she

went, Kyle debated whether to tamp down their fire or build it up even higher. He finally opted to bank it into a slow-burning glow that would discourage four-footed predators and, if necessary, warn off any night-time travelers who (hopefully) would prefer to remain unseen. Before slipping out of his shirt and jeans and sliding into the open sleeping bag with Wren, Kyle placed their hiking staffs within easy reach.

Skin to skin in the cozy warmth of the tent, Wren ran her hands down Kyle's smooth back and hungrily sought his lips. When he brushed her breasts lightly, her relaxation changed to receptive delight. Crushed up against him, Wren felt Kyle's arousal against her thighs and smiled in the dark.

Awakening somewhat later, Wren strained to identify night sounds outside their thin tent wall. She stiffened when she detected some stealthy crackles and munching in the underbrush.

"Foraging deer," Kyle muttered drowsily.

After the deer had drunk from the spring and moved on, Wren fell into an uneasy slumber haunted by dreams of hidden watchers.

CHAPTER TWO

A misting rain had doused their fire by morning. When Wren and Kyle wakened in the gray light, they were unaware of a dark form squatting some distance up the path from their tent site. Memories of the previous night's pleasures and the comfort of cuddling in the warmth of the sleeping bag suggested they linger before starting another day on the trail. This was their honeymoon after all.

But when Kyle unzipped their tent flap for a better assessment of the weather, he glimpsed the humped shadow further up the trail where, he recalled with a surge of fear, no obstacle had stood the night before. Focusing more deliberately, Kyle made out a broad-brimmed hat pulled low over a gray poncho that shrouded the unmoving shape. A long something that could be either a gun or a staff leaned casually against it.

Nudging Wren, Kyle whispered, "Look over there."

The strain in Kyle's voice alerted Wren and she rolled over slowly until she, too, could stare up the dim path. As she did so, the figure in the poncho rose and walked silently away, still cradling the long, dark object. As it disappeared into the mist, Wren squeezed Kyle's hand. "What the hell was that?"

Kyle tugged his nose nervously. "A person, no doubt," he ventured, "but man or woman? And more to the point, what was he or she carrying?"

Wren shook her head. Tales of "shoot first, ask questions later" mountaineers surged through her mind along with stories of fugitives evading the law for years by hiding out in these wild, largely uncharted areas of the Smokies.

Crawling shakily out of their low tent, Wren fumbled through their gear. When she dropped the coffeepot, its clatter echoed about the fog-shrouded glen.

"Oh good, Wren," Kyle gibed, "let's call everyone in for breakfast."

They waited anxiously but no other sounds intruded on the dripping silence except the chirps of awakening birds. With one eye on the path ahead, they continued their morning routine of breakfast and packing up. When they began hiking, Kyle's inner alarms had calmed somewhat. An invisible sun brightened the mists swirling about them. Even so, they could see only a few yards ahead of them.

Slowly they crunched past cobwebs glittering with dew and heard unseen birds warbling from shadowy trees. Stirred to her core by the serene beauty they walked through, Wren was silent, wondering how she could feel so at home in surroundings unlike anything she had ever experienced. Perhaps it was Kyle's comfort in the woods rubbing off on her? She slanted her eye up at the sturdy man by her side. What a strange expression played across his normally impassive face!

"It's odd," Kyle mused aloud, "I feel certain we are going to meet something unlikely up the trail, something or someone we can't evade." He reached for Wren's hand and kissed it gently. Wren curled her fingers around Kyle's thumb in a gesture of child-like confidence that, once again, stirred all Kyle's protective instincts.

15

A happiness that almost ached surged through Wren, stinging tears from her eyes. She caressed a laurel leaf, silvery with dew, and licked the drops from her fingertips. Holding hands like two children in a fairy tale, Wren and Kyle pressed through the hazy shrubs looming around them. Wren's reverie broke when Kyle slowly tightened his grip and pulled her to his side. Something was different. Now Wren sensed it, too.

No longer were they surrounded by shadowy bushes and dripping trees. An eerie sense of space enveloped them. Looking down, they saw that the cinder path was merging into evenly spaced ties with gray mist curling up between them. From far below echoed sounds of churning waters. They were enveloped by a bright cloud that swaddled the mountain.

Wren's knees began to quiver, a familiar reaction to heights, and a hollowness hit her dead center. Rotating carefully in place, she looked back but could barely discern shapes in the mist. The fog was thicker here where the ground fell sharply away. Dizziness sickened her.

Kyle peered ahead intently but now could see less than a yard. Even his own feet were barely visible. "I think we are on a trestle bridge," he hazarded.

"A-argh, " croaked Wren with rising panic. "Kyle, where does it go? Is it safe? What shape is it in? What if this is where the tracks got washed out?"

"There's one way to find out," Kyle suggested with more calm than he felt.

Wren's eyes widened, "Oh, no. Oh, no. I'm staying right here!"

"Okay, then. I'll go on ahead and then come back if it's safe."

"Un, huh! Leave me here alone while you disappear? No way!"

"Well, then, what? We can't just stand here." "Can we go

back and wait for the fog to pass?"

"That might be hours from now," Kyle observed. "It may be easier to cross this trestle if we can't see all the way down. I suspect I'd never get you across here in clear daylight," he added with a wry grin.

Hugging Wren closely, he murmured softly into her hair, "One way or another, honey, we have to get across if we are to find Lovada Cove."

Wren gnawed her knuckles, pondering their options. Kyle had a point about the possible advantage of not knowing how high they were. On the other hand, they didn't know how long this trestle was or how safe.

"I don't like this at all, Kyle."

Kyle could feel her trembling as she pressed against him and pitied her terror. If he couldn't get her to move soon, she might freak out altogether.

"Wren," he began gently, "Wren, listen to me. We both want to get to Lovada Cove. And this is the only way in that we know..."

"No one ever mentioned a trestle," Wren protested weakly.

"They didn't," Kyle granted. "But obviously there are people who come and go across it. Remember the signs we saw along the trail?"

"Maybe others can do it ....I'm not sure I can."

"Of course you can, hon. You've never yet allowed anything to stop you going after something you've set your heart on."

"But we could be killed doing this!" Wren blurted. She bit her lip, pushed her hair back from her face, peered behind her and then ahead over Kyle's shoulder. Her palms were damp with sweat. If she gave in to her fears now, she suspected she might never again have this chance to search for her roots. If she didn't cross, she might regret it the rest of her life.

17

With a deep sigh, Wren mumbled, "Oh, hell! Kyle, turn around and go ahead of me. I'll hang on to your pack." She grasped the straps on Kyle's pack, drew a shuddering breath and when he looked over his shoulder at her, nodded reluctantly.

"Ata' girl!" Kyle cheered her stoutly. "I'll check the ties ahead with the stick as we go along. If I run into nothing, we'll just turn around and go back."

Wren moaned, "Don't you dare find nothing, Kyle Makepeace!"

Only her sore knees kept Wren from suggesting they crawl as Kyle began to tap his way forward like a blind man. The further out they went, the more silent it became, as the mist snaked around them, now thicker, now thinning slightly. Wren's ears felt like they were stuffed with cotton. Occasionally, Kyle would warn Wren that a certain tie was slippery. Suddenly he stopped and Wren bumped into him.

"What is it?"

Kyle took a deep breath and emitted a wild keening cry of sheer exhilaration.

"Damn your Cherokee blood," she croaked, "you're actually enjoying this!"

The echoes were quickly muffled by the fog and Kyle began walking cautiously forward again on the dripping ties. Wren held firmly to the straps of his pack and followed behind, hoping her now active anger would neutralize her terror.

All at once, she heard a crunching sound and realized it was Kyle's boots hitting gravel. They were across! How long had it taken them? Wren was sure it was an hour; Kyle countered it was less than ten minutes. A glance at her watch confirmed his estimate.

However, even Kyle was glad to take a break before hiking on. As they rested their packs on the ground and munched on some granola bars, the pervasive mist began to burn away and they could see some distance further

The Trestle Bridge

down the trail. But when Wren turned back to study the trestle they had crossed, it remained swathed in cloud as if a door had closed behind them.

They shouldered their packs knowing they had reached a point of no return, of having entered a new, yet somehow familiar, country. The trail took them around a long sloping curve and into a gentle descent. After some time, they encountered a stretch of trail where the banks above and below them were scarred from a massive rock slide.

The trail itself continued, firm and level, as if deliberately refashioned out of the debris. There was only one obvious explanation. But for some reason, this evidence of human presence no longer surprised them. They had begun to suspect that there were people living back here, probably for reasons as dark as the ravines they were skirting.

Their fears of the previous night were unaccountably gone, however, and both Wren and Kyle experienced a pervasive sense of security and well-being.

"There shall be no harm or ruin on all my holy mountain" Kyle quoted under his breath.

"Say what?" Wren queried.

"Oh, just a line I remember from an ancient prophecy," Kyle hedged.

"Hmm?" Wren invited but Kyle said no more.

They trekked on together. Once again holding hands as they walked through a garden of blooming laurel, rhododendron and swaying trilliums. Lacy shade from huge hemlocks dappled their path. A splash of bright orange caught Kyle's eye. He peered through a break in the laurel and pulled Wren to a halt.

"Flame azalea." he whispered, "it's rare to see such a full stand." They paused to absorb the orange-red splendor blooming in an open space among the trees and, at this moment, highlighted by sunrays slanting through the thinning mist. Something straight and dark jutted up in the glade just beyond the flowering shrubs.

"What is that?" Wren asked, startled. "A dead tree?"

"Let's see," Kyle suggested. They turned off the trail and plunged through the laurel thicket towards the sunlight. A narrow deer path led them directly into a grassy area where spreading patches of daffodil and narcissi leaves crowded wild iris that were just coming into bloom. The dark shape turned out to be a chimney, the smoke-blackened remnant of a burned-out cabin. Large blocks of stone, now covered with moss and ivy, lay tumbled around it. A closer look revealed they were tombstones, all crudely etched with the same date. Many of them were too worn to read but it looked like most bore the same family name. Wren felt a sudden chill as if a thin cloud had passed across the sun.

Kyle noticed her shiver so when he discovered the doorsill of the house that had belonged to the chimney, he playfully mounted it and pretended to knock on the door. "Anyone to home?" he inquired.

"Welcome to the Bentley homeplace," a voice sang out from the woods.

Old Bentley Place

CHAPTER THREE

Wren squealed and Kyle whirled around, his staff at the ready. A short figure swathed in a gray poncho stepped into the glade carrying the wide-brimmed hat they recognized from their early morning apparition. Gray braids fell over its shoulders, framing a brown face wizened as an old apple. Golden eyes regarded them solemnly.

"Ah'm Mencie," she responded to their unspoken question, "and you'ns are....?"

"Kyle and Wren Makepeace" Kyle replied, his easy manner masking his native wariness.

Mencie nodded. Wren, uneasily eyeing this mountain gnome with the imperial manner, suspected this was not news to her.

Mencie flashed a brief glance at Wren before she answered
Kyle's next question. "Yes, I live here abouts ... in the place fer which you're bound."

Kyle and Wren exchanged startled looks. "How ...?"

Mencie held up her hand. "No one comes to Lovada Cove less'n they is Sent or Summoned. We've been waitin' on you. Follow me, if you please."

Although the request was courteous, Wren and Kyle knew that Mencie's words were an order. Chills chased

23

themselves up Wren's spine, followed by a flare of resentment. She did not like the way this person was assuming control of her life. As they followed Mencie along a narrow trail, Wren pondered the cool gleam in the old woman's eyes. Mica winking in the wind-scoured granite of the mountain would be less intimidating. Wren's chin tilted higher.

A glance at Kyle walking cautiously at her side confirmed that he, too, was troubled and uneasy. He kept a firm grip on the walking stick he'd been carrying as a surrogate weapon. "A witchy sort of thing, isn't she?" Wren murmured. Kyle nodded moodily. He had recognized in Mencie a presence he both feared and reverenced. It was never safe to encounter one of her kind.

The trail was widening, becoming more road-like. A weathered cabin stood to one side and Mencie nodded to two men stacking wood near it. "Freeman. Hall."

"Mencie," they acknowledged, before turning back to their work.

"The Garenflo brothers," Mencie informed Wren and Kyle. They passed two more dwellings as the road led them further into an expansive cove where green pastures, separated by low walls of stacked stone, spread up the slopes. Here and there, kitchen gardens sprouted a variety of corn and vegetables. Some elderly people were carefully pulling honeycombs from beehives set back behind one of the houses. The whole scene only served to heighten Wren and Kyle's apprehensions for they were walking into a community that shouldn't be there.

"Is this place real?" Wren whispered, echoing Kyle's doubts.

"Oh, it's real," Kyle replied carefully. "I'm just wondering how *safe* it might be. What if this cove is really a ...," he licked dry lips, "really a coven?"

Wren's eyes widened in alarm.

Mencie turned on them as she caught their whispered exchange. With a faint smile, she said, "No, Wren and Kyle, it's not safe. It's good ... for most who come here. But safe? Ah, no."

Wren stopped in her tracks. "Where are you taking us?" she demanded.

"Up to Oma's place," Mencie replied cheerfully.

"So who is Oma?" Kyle challenged.

"She puts up the visitors," Mencie explained.

"You get many?" Kyle asked incredulously.

"Guess you could say that. As ah've mentioned, only those come here who are Sent ... like you are," Mencie replied, giving Kyle a sharp look, "or Summoned, like you, Winnie Lovada." She smiled tightly when Wren started at hearing her birth name.

Mencie opened a low gate and led them up a flagstone walkway edged with primroses. Kyle snorted, "Well, Wren, looks like we are being led up that proverbial primrose path!"

Startled, Wren glanced down and muttered, "I don't believe any of this!"

They were approaching a large house with an old-fashioned porch running along two sides. A voice rang out.

"Bring'em round to the kitchen, Mencie. Ah'm jest fixin' to set out dinner."

Kyle and Wren eased their packs off and left them on the porch. They stepped into a large kitchen where at a wood burning cook stove, a stout woman in bib overalls and bare feet was ladling stew from a large pot. Wisps of iron gray hair escaped the thick bun on her neck and curled about her flushed cheeks.

She turned as they entered, dark eyes gleaming kindly, "Kyle. Winnie. Good to have you with us. We've set out your places." And she nodded toward a round table near a bay window. Too dazed by now to ask any more questions,

Wren and Kyle obediently stood by the chairs indicated. Two denim-clad men entered the kitchen from another room and helped Oma carry the stew and cornbread to the table where a huge bowl of salad already rested. Mencie opened the thick door of the "cold safe" and took out a pewter pitcher that she positioned carefully in the center of the table.

"Meet Jonah," she announced, indicating the taller man with the long white beard. Jonah nodded, his blue eyes assessing them keenly. His glance sharpened as his gaze fell on Kyle and a smile touched his lips but he said nothing.

'This one here is Anson Jack," Oma leaned toward a wiry, sunburnt man who looked like he had spent most of his life wrestling a plow. The companionable glance he gave Oma suggested a lifetime shared.

Mencie placed a small white napkin at Jonah's right but he shook his head briefly and she quietly removed it. This interchange, however, caught Kyle's attention and further provoked the uneasy intuition that he was known here far better than he wished. He looked curiously at the table. A golden liquid glimmered in the pewter jug; the cornbread loaf lay unbroken beside it. For a moment, powerful memories threatened to break through the barriers he had set upon them. Struggling to subdue his rush of feeling, Kyle glanced at the others. No one but Jonah seemed to be paying him any particular attention. Wren, however, felt Kyle tensing and her own anxiety mounted.

At an invitation from Oma, everyone at the table joined hands. Kyle's palm felt sweaty to her touch and Wren knew something was seriously distressing her husband.

"God of life and Guide for all who seek," Oma began softly, "we welcome Kyle and Winnie to this table. May our sharing in this gift of your bounty strengthen all of us to accept your call and do what is required of us."

In the brief silence before those at table raised their

bowed heads, Wren and Kyle felt themselves embraced by a tenderness that momentarily disarmed all their fears. A quiet peace calmed the unease within them and they were content to leave their questions unanswered for the moment.

The rich aroma from the stew pot drifted past Wren and she discovered she was ravenous. Oma ladled out the stew while Jonah dished up salads with flair. At this table, the common act of eating together carried a significance Wren felt but could not name. A comfortable conversation about the spring crops sprang up among the four older folk, giving Kyle and Wren a chance to relax and to observe them.

Although they were all obviously of retirement age or beyond, they exuded a youthful vigor. Anson Jack's hands were gnarled from years of heavy work but Jonah's tapered fingers resembled those of a scholar. Oma made sure all plates were filled, padding back and forth between the cupboards and the table with butter from the cold safe and more cornbread as the first loaf disappeared.

As no one questioned their presence, Kyle and Wren began to wonder anew about the apparent expectation of their arrival. Wren's edginess returned but true to form, she put off inquiring about things whose answers she had reason to dread. Kyle kept his eyes on his plate, eating deliberately and silently. At least one person at this table had known him in another life and Kyle didn't want to invite any probing conversation, friendly or otherwise.

Abruptly, Mencie lifted her head and raised her hand. The others at table fell silent. A moment later, she announced, "They're a'comin'!" She grabbed her gray-brimmed hat and rushed out of the kitchen while Oma, Anson Jack and Jonah began to clear the table hurriedly. Mystified, Kyle and Wren joined them. Somewhere in the distance, the musical howling of the vanished red wolf echoed.

Oma's Kitchen

25

Oma laughed delightedly and patted her gray bun. 'Those boys ... I declare. You'd think they'd know the wolves only answer them of an evenin'. Still," she cocked her head listening critically, "they sound pretty good. Guess they remember somethin'." Oma' cheeks were rosy as she hurried outside to join Anson Jack and numerous other folks converging on the dirt road that led further up The Cove. Jonah strolled into another room.

Uncertain what to do next, Kyle and Wren opted to follow Anson Jack and Oma. As they hurried to catch up with the men and women clad in faded work clothes who were converging on the dusty road from all directions, Kyle grasped Wren's elbow. "Do you notice something peculiar about all these folks?"

"There's plenty of peculiar things here, Kyle. What are you referring to?"

"Nearly everyone here looks to be over sixty. I don't see a younger person in the group."

"And not a single child!" Wren added.

Just as they topped a rise, the air was suddenly filled with screams and shrill cries as dozens of children surged across a field. "Mamaw! Papaw!" the young horde hollered as they rushed into the open arms of eagerly waiting men and women.

"What IS this?" Kyle muttered to Wren. "It looks like a giant family reunion!"

"You might call it that," replied a voice behind them. Mencie, panting and smiling, came up to them. "It's Homecoming. Every year when the mountain laurel blooms, our young'uns come back to the homeplace. Like you'ns," she added.

Out in the field, family groups were forming and reforming as more people with camping gear poured through a notch across the valley. Children ran about screaming wildly; teenagers greeted one another, boys hooting and shoving

29

as they leaped over the low stone walls, girls chattering like squirrels. Parents followed a step behind, eager to greet the various elders hurrying past Wren and Kyle.

"Hey, Mencie," shouted a few from a group that surged by them. She flapped her hat at them. "Some of Oma's kin. They live over near Knoxville and make it back most every year. My own? Back up yonder." Mencie tilted her chin toward a grassy cemetery on a rise behind a steepled white church.

Wren watched the trilled greetings and joyous bear hugs wistfully, pain and anger twisting a familiar knife in her heart. Kyle pitied her as she scanned every female face, seeking that spark of recognition she'd dreamed of for over thirty years; that smile of welcome that despite all her self-talk, she still hoped to see.

When Kyle gently drew her against his body, Wren murmured , "I just can't get past it ... hoping that she'll come back, looking for me, wanting me ..." Angrily she brushed tears away with the back of her hand. "It's too late for that now. Why did I ever come here?"

A boney hand suddenly grasped her wrist. "You came, honey," Mencie said, "'cause your old Granny is still alive and stompin'." Wren blinked at the gnome-like countenance, startled by those odd golden eyes that twinkled back at her.

"See there," Mencie pointed, "that's Zettie over yonder. Zettie Lovada, "she added significantly.

Wren followed her gaze and picked out a tiny white-haired lady cuddling a baby that a hovering young mother had placed in her arms.

Confronting Wren's puzzled frown, Mencie continued, "We know who you are, child. No one is forgotten at the Homeplace. Come on now. Zettie's wantin' to see you ... Bin wantin' and waitin' for nigh over thirty years."

Plucking Wren's sleeve, Mencie pulled her out of Kyle's grasp and led her across the grass to a group gathered in the shade of a huge oak.

"Zettie! Zettie Lovada," she sang out. "Look who ah'm bringin' you."

The bright-eyed little woman looked up, her gaze traveling over Wren eagerly. Handing the baby back to its mother, she walked slowly toward Wren, tenderness suffusing her face. "Are my eyes tellin' me true? You're my Della's girl, Winnie Lovada, come home at last?" Wren found herself gathered in an embrace that touched the emptiness at her core that even Kyle's love had not filled. She made no effort now to blink back the tears that rushed to her eyes as she laid her face against the soft white hair of her Mamaw.

During the long wordless embrace, conflicting emotions battled within Wren. Surprise, wonder, anger, pain, all vied for recognition. Pulling back, Wren regarded the lined face of the older woman and struggled with a lifetime of disappointed hopes. Under Zettie's soft gaze, she felt her defenses crumbling.

"Oh, Mamaw," cried out the five-year-old in Wren, "why did she go away? Why did she leave me? Didn't she want me? Didn't she love me? What did I do wrong? I kept watching for her to come... but she never did." Wren paused for breath, a catch in her throat. Slowly she lowered her head and admitted in a hoarse whisper: "I guess I wasn't good enough...."

Zettie pulled Wren close again, rocking and singing some wordless lullaby as sobs racked Wren's body. "Child, child," she murmured, "If only I could have taken all your pain myself; taken it away from you, darling beautiful child." Tears coursed down the cheek she laid against Wren's.

"Della loved you, honey. I'm sure of that."

Wren stiffened and her eyes turned briefly stony. "She sure chose an odd way to show it, Mamaw! No mother should, could do what she did!"

31

Kyle stood by feeling like an intruder at this intimate scene. His wife now belonged to others, and was not just his alone. It was hard to accept that he might no longer be the most important per- son in her life. Slowly the two women, arms entwined, walked across the meadow toward a weathered cabin further up the road. Kyle watched them go, desolation tinged with envy, sweeping over him. Mencie touched his arm. "Go along with them. Winnie will need you now more than ever."

"Will she?" Kyle wondered, tasting a jealousy that dismayed him even as it shamed him.

By the time Kyle reached the cabin, Zettie had already settled Wren in a chair on the porch and was bustling back out through the door with three steaming mugs of tea. Wren slumped, dazed, in the wicker rocker, not even acknowledging Kyle as he took a chair at her side. Zettie handed Wren a mug. She sipped slowly and lowered it to her lap. For a while, the three of them rocked in silence, each caught in her or his own struggle.

Kyle studied Zettie out of the corner of his eye, seeking points of resemblance between the older woman and Wren. Both were of slender build with a natural grace of movement that made Zettie appear much younger than her seventy some years. Although softened by time, the structure of Zettie's face mirrored Wren's piquant features so strikingly that Kyle felt he was seeing a vision of his wife as she might appear on their fiftieth wedding anniversary.

The firm set of their chins bespoke a stubbornness very familiar to Kyle. But whereas Zettie's lined features were tranquil with a wisdom acquired from years of struggle, Wren's face was eloquent as waves of emotion succeeded one another. Hurt, longing, wonder and hope played across Wren's mobile features. Kyle noted her firmly compressed lips and knew she was more upset by the fast pace of events, developments that threatened her sense of control, than by the facts themselves. Wisely, Kyle decided to remain silent lest he attract a swift flash of Wren's volatile temper only too familiar to him.

With a gentle sigh, Zettie balanced her empty mug on the porch rail and ran her gnarled fingers along the seam of her faded housedress. "You'n wantin' me to tell you about Della, aren't you, Winnie? Wantin' me to explain why she did what she did?" she asked softly.

Wren shifted toward Zettie, hope lifting her shoulders.

Zettie's faded blue eyes caught Wren gazing out across the pastures toward the notch where people were still entering the cove. "If'n I could, I would, honey, I most surely would. But I've not found the answer myself in all these years. Though she was my only girl, we weren't close. She seemed to come up so fast, old before her time." Zettie frowned, remembering things the meaning of which she had never dared to explore.

"Della was barely of an age when she left Clyde and me, too early I guess. We were livin' up above Viney Branch, then, where we had a farm and fields. 'Tweren't enough to keep us even then, so while Clyde tended the cows and 'bacca, I taught in the schoolhouse where all the young'uns from Viney Branch started out. Maybe I wasn't home enough ... maybe I asked too much of Della, she bein' the only girl with the two boys ..." Zettie paused, old regret deepening the creases around her eyes.

Though still silent, Wren had stopped rocking. She leaned forward, her knuckles white around the mug balanced on her knees, while she stared fixedly at Zettie's silhouette.

"Viney Branch?" Kyle asked quizzically. "I thought you were from here."

Zettie nodded, "I was born here in Lovada Cove but after the trains stopped comin' in, it was no place to raise a family. Clyde 'n me left 'long with the others who were Sent Out. The Elders stayed and we came back with our

Karen Karper Fredette

Zettie's Front Porch

34

young'uns as often as we could. Della always loved it and she came along while she was livin' at home. But after she started workin' over in Black Mountain in the craft shops, she said she just couldn't find her way back any more. Clyde 'n me, we felt bad but it happens to most of us at one time or another so we didn't throw it up to her." "Then one day she came home and told us she was pregnant and scared 'cause she'd lost her job and her man had moved on.

'Course we wanted her to stay with us but she wouldn't. We gave her what little cash money we had laid by. She took it and went to Lashton. She wrote only once after that, telling us that she'd had a baby girl that she'd named Winnie Lovada, after my own Maw."

Wren clutched her mug convulsively, questions hovering on her lips. "Where'd she go then?"

I wish I knew, hon, I wish I knew. Clyde 'n me watched and waited for her until it was time for us to come back here. Even here, I still watched. I've kept the last dress I was makin' for her, and Clyde wrote a letter to give her when he knew was dyin'. I don't know but what she just never could find her way back through the mists.

Sometimes I think I hear her cryin' out there, wantin' to come back. Oh, yes, she hurt us bad but I 'spect it ain't nothin' like the hurt she herself carried."

Zettie reached over and caressed Wren's twitching hands. "I need to tell you somethin', Winnie girl. Clyde 'n me couldn't come back here ourselves until we looked past our own hurt and forgave her ... until we agreed that the only thing God asked us to do was to just go on lovin' her. Honey, I'm ready to throw a party for her today ... should she come!"

Wren's fingers twitched in Zettie's grasp. "Would she want me, even now?"

A thick silence absorbed Wren's words, words flung out

in mindless hurt. Zettie caught her breath sharply, "More than ever, baby, more than ever." Wren still stared across the meadow, oblivious to the tears coursing down her cheeks.

Slowly Zettie resumed rocking, her hands now open, unmoving on her lap. Kyle felt the same tenderness surround them as they'd felt in Oma's kitchen and knew that Zettie was praying.

Little by little some of the conflict drained out of Wren. "How can I forgive her if I don't know why? If I'll never know?" Zettie's chair creaked rhythmically.

"She may well be dead by now," Wren added sadly, the hopes of a lifetime dying within her soul.

Zettie nodded. "Maybe she sent you to tell me that she's gone. Soon as I saw you, child, I gave up my last hope of seeing her again."

The meadow was silent now, the shadows of the western mountains stretching across it. Zettie's porch still glowed in the last rays of the sun beaming through the notch. Kyle watched a few low clouds, their undersides aflame, and his heart burned within him.

His own anger at Wren's mother surprised him. He felt as if he could almost hate this woman who had hurt Wren, Zettie and others so deeply. But as often as Kyle glanced at the petite elder, he could detect no bitterness, no lingering resentment. Only a gentle sadness rested on her tranquil features.

"I had hoped that she ..." Wren lifted her hands and dropped them despairingly. "... hoped that she would love me." She struggled to pull a handkerchief from her jeans until Kyle offered her one from his hip pocket.

Zettie cupped her hands as if gathering Wren's pain and lift- ing it up to a God who was no stranger to suffering or rejection. After a few moments, she turned toward the confused younger woman.

"Winnie, hon," she began, "can you go on living with your questions for now?"

Wren's head jerked up. "No-o-o," she began, paused as if re-assessing her feelings, and admitted, "Maybe if there's some of the answers here." She eyed Zettie hopefully.

"I'll give you all I have," Zettie promised softly.

Wren nodded, suspecting too little, too late. But perhaps enough? Her heart felt lighter, already less burdened with lingering anger at a woman who, much younger than she, had chosen life for her child.

Kyle, eyeing the gathering dusk, rose slowly and held out his hand to Zettie. "I'm glad we met you." He groped for something more to say as Wren stepped hesitantly into Zettie's open arms.

'I'm sorry for your pain," he added awkwardly, bending to kiss her wrinkled cheek. "And Wren's, too."

Zettie nodded as they stepped off the porch. "Give us time, Kyle... and God give you courage," she added suddenly, her hand lifting slightly.

Arrested by her words, Wren looked back toward the porch. In the failing light, it was hard to make out the expression on the old woman's face but it seemed to be a blend of compassion and yearning, directed toward Wren first of all, but embracing Kyle as well. "Mamaw," Wren mouthed silently before turning swiftly away.

As he hurried after Wren, Kyle wondered if Zettie had guessed his stirrings of jealousy. "Yes, she likely did," he thought, his shame relieved by the instant realization that she had also understood, accepted and forgiven him. Twilight had settled over the cove once the sun had dropped behind the mountains across the valley.

Wren and Kyle reclaimed the packs they had dropped on Oma's porch, now dimly lit by the rising moon and the glow of a lantern someone had thoughtfully set out on a ledge. As they were helping one another don the heavy backpacks and discussing where to pitch camp that night, Mencie materialized out of the gloom.

"And where do you think you are going?" she demanded.

"What does it matter to you?" Wren countered rudely.

"We're free to find some privacy, aren't we?" Kyle stopped, his desire to protect Wren warring with the instinctual apprehension he felt in Mencie's presence.

"Yeh'm," Mencie murmured softly, "a lot's beginnin' fer ya. We need you here for a time before you can be Sent Out. Kyle, Jonah wants a word with you. How about tomorrow mornin' at the chapel?"

Wren noted the wary surprise on Kyle's face, and new questions wakened in her heart.

Mencie touched Wren's cheek tenderly and despite herself, Wren began to weep. "Oh, damn! Seems like all I do around here is cry."

"Why don't you two camp at the Bentley homeplace where I first kotched up with you?" Mencie suggested. "None of their kin return anymore so you'ns won't be bothered out there. There's an old dipper by the spring not ten feet from the chimney-pile. See you'ns in the mornin'."

"Meddling old bitch!" Wren muttered as she stumbled down the road ahead of Kyle.

"Bitch or witch?" Kyle wondered uneasily as he hitched up his pack and warily followed his wife, the hairs on his neck tingling again.

CHAPTER FOUR

Songs and laughter from various campfires drifted toward them as Wren and Kyle hurried along the path leading out of the cove. The windows in the Garonflo brothers' house glowed with soft light and they heard but could not see, people conversing quietly on the front porch. But soon the only light other than the fire- flies flitting along their path was from the lantern Mencie had thrust into Kyle's hand.

By the time they found the Bentley place, trailers of mist had started to wind around them. When Kyle and Wren opened their packs to set up camp, they found that someone had added a food packet to their gear plus a thermos of herb tea. Kyle sniffed it cautiously but when he could detect nothing more than chamomile and mint, he and Wren drank it gratefully, the warmth welcome as the chill of late May in the mountains deepened with the darkness. Gradually they relaxed in the glow of their campfire and allowed the tensions of the day to sort themselves out.

Cupping her cheeks in her hands, Wren rested her elbows on her bent knees and studied the flames. "Well," she observed shakily, "we found Lovada Cove, didn't we!"

"I believe it found us," Kyle mused somberly. He turned to Wren. "I'm not sure what our options will be in the morning. I don't really care about this talk with Jonah."

Touched by his obvious conflicts, Wren reached over to rest her hand on Kyle's knee as she stared into the fire.

'Tm not sure what I want anymore," she replied softly. "Part of me wants to run like hell. This place scares me... and these people! There's something so unreal about all this ... it has the feel of a dream that could turn into a nightmare at any moment. I'm all torn up inside." She laughed shakily. "At the same time, I'm feeling lighter, freer maybe. It's like things that have been tied up in a tight bundle in the back of a dark closet have been jerked out, shook up... and tossed around. I...I don't know how to put all these pieces together ... or if I can ... or if I should."

Wren's voice trailed off into the rhythmic pulsing of peepers and tree frogs in the deep woods surrounding them. She and Kyle both jumped when a whip-poor-will sounded off under a shrub just beyond their tent.

"God, I forgot how loud those things can be!" Kyle exclaimed irritably. They heard another one call further off in the forest and leaves rustled as their neighbor took flight. From further away, a yipping and howling drifted toward them on the night breeze.

"If I didn't know that red wolves were extinct in these parts, I would swear that's what we are hearing," Kyle muttered, cocking his ear in the direction of the sound. "It's definitely not coyotes, too musical and deep. I wonder what else has found refuge back here that no one knows about?"

Wren whispered, "Kyle, I'm scared! These people ... this place... it's so unnatural, isn't it? Maybe the sooner we leave, the better ... this place is just too weird."

"Yeh," admitted Kyle, grateful that Wren had expressed his own fears. "This whole damned set-up doesn't make sense. But," he paused to formulate his impressions, I'm not sure we can just walk away now."

"Kyle! What do you mean? They can't stop us, can they?" "Well, not physically, of course..." Kyle voiced his thoughts reluctantly. "Wren, these folk know who we are; seem to know more about us than we know about ourselves. You are Winnie Lovada now ... and for what it's worth, I feel certain they're expecting something of you." Wren's body jerked in surprise.

"What's this about you, Kyle?" Wren challenged, remembering Jonah's apparent recognition of her husband and Kyle's strange distress. 'They seem to know things about you that even I don't."

Kyle stiffened, unwanted memories assailing him. Silently he wrapped his arms about Wren's bowed shoulders and laid his cheek against her coppery hair. She could feel the pulse in his throat thumping erratically as he struggled for control. The night winds played about them more strongly, tugging at their tent ropes and swirling a damp fog through the clearing. A chill that the leaping campfire could not dissipate swept over them.

Somewhere in the night, someone was playing a reed flute, the plaintive tones rising and falling on the wind. It sounded so ghostly that Wren glanced about, wondering what it meant. Kyle didn't wonder. He knew. Deep in his Cherokee soul he felt himself being lured into the spirit world and he automatically resisted, as he had so often in the past. Instinct warned him they were camping on sacred ground where spirits roamed. Suddenly he was resenting Mencie who had suggested they spend this night in what he now knew (and she *surely* knew), were the Borderlands.

Kyle's nails dug into Wren's shoulder as the keening of the reed flute grew wilder and he whispered, "Don't move. Don't say anything. No matter what happens, stay still."

Their campfire dimmed as phantom fingers of mists

crept into the glade. The shuffling of many weary feet filled their ears and the glade seemed crowded with a host of ragged figures, gaunt people who crouched and moved with utmost stealth. Even the children with the large mournful eyes were unnaturally quiet. Wren groped for the silver disk between her breasts.

Men with bows faced outward toward the trees while the women and children gathered close about an ancient One in the center of the glade. Suddenly Wren understood what was happening. These people were Cherokee, desperate survivors of the nation that had once inhabited all these mountains. These haunted figures were fleeing from hunters who sought to herd them into stockades and then force them westward, away from these mountains, away from these coves and hunting grounds that had been theirs to roam for generations beyond count.

Beside her, Kyle sucked in his breath as the Old One stood, and with eyes closed, lifted his head as if sniffing the wind. Slowly he turned. Kyle's heart thumped. He and Wren were discovered. Advancing toward them, the Elder raised his spear high, ready to thrust them through where they huddled, unable to stir. Kyle felt his mind being probed, his life being weighed in a balance. Summoning all his courage, Kyle looked up into the regal, ravaged face above them and strange words came out of his mouth. He pointed toward the break in the undergrowth through which Mencie had led them earlier that day.

The Elder growled and shook his spear, questioning Kyle's right to direct them. Carefully, Kyle reached inside his shirt and withdrew a fringed pouch, sweat-stained and shabby. He held it up so the Ancient One could see it clearly. Regarding Kyle steadily, the Elder took it into his gnarled fingers and sniffed it. He returned it to Kyle with a nod and grunt of approval. Swiftly he herded his people toward the dark opening in the brush, the warriors following last on silent feet.

The mist thickened, obliterating all sound. As silence enveloped her, Wren lifted her head. She felt cold and realized that Kyle wasn't with her. He had disappeared along with the ghostly throng. "He is leading his people to a safe haven," she thought, not even questioning how she knew this.

"He'll be back," the trees whispered but Wren was not com- forted. She knew he would not return the same man who had walked into Lovada Cove with her. Something buried deep in him was being awakened and she dreaded what that portended, afraid she would lose Kyle to something or someone with a prior claim on him.

As Wren continued to huddle in the chill fog, clutching the pendant under her shirt, a strange drowsiness took hold of her. A woman came toward her, lifted her from the ground and carried her like a child toward the burnt out shell of the Bentley home- stead. No longer a ruin, it was now restored. The child that was Wren but not Wren, was settled on a blanket by the hearth.

Dreamily, Wren watched as the woman shushed the child's fear and removed her torn clothing, fingering the small disk threaded on a chain about the child's neck. Sadness played across the woman's features as she slipped into a rocker, cuddling the child, now become an infant, against her belly. Slowly she rocked and chanted, repeating phrases over and over as if she hoped to impress them on the infant's developing brain.

The mesmerizing song continued until the child disappeared from Wren's sight, covered by a loose, shabby smock. Profound distress invaded Wren, communicated by this now pregnant young woman who seemed so vulnerable and alone. Whenever her anxieties overtook her, the woman would begin the chant again as if it were her only defense against the dread that hung over her and the child in her womb.

At one point, the woman rose heavily from the chair and plucked a vial of dark liquid from the table. She pulled the stop- per from the small bottle and sniffed it, indecision flickering in her eyes. "One swallow would be enough," she murmured.

In her wraith-like state, Wren could see and hear but felt herself helpless to intervene. However, she felt threatened, agitated, as if her life depended on the unborn child's survival. The fetus stirred in response to Wren's distress and the woman automatically placed her hand over her bulging womb. Tears coursed down her wan features and she wavered, sighed, and finally stoppered the bottle.

Drearily the woman slumped back into the rocker and, resting her hands on her belly, took up her insistent chanting of a heartfelt mantra: I must live, I must live. Wren could smell the woman's distress even more strongly than the acrid scent from the bottle. This conflict, this slight vein of energy, was her only hope of rescuing the pallid woman and her unborn child.

In her trance-like state, Wren felt a profound kinship with the pregnant woman, but she did not know who she was nor what begot her near-despair. Before Wren could say or do anything else, the room began to grow hazy and dissolve. Cool air brushed her cheek and she found herself struggling against the restraint of two strong arms.

"Wren. Wren." Kyle's voice reached her from a great distance. Torn between her desperate need to help the woman and her love for Kyle that was pulling her away, Wren thrashed briefly before her eyes flew open.

She found herself once more in the glade surrounding the Bentley home place. Kyle was holding her tightly where she stood within the tumbled foundation stones of the old cabin. The worried look in his dark eyes mirrored her own distress. When Kyle saw that Wren could walk on her own, he led her back to their campsite. Gently, he rubbed her hand, still cramped from gripping the silver disk.

"Kyle, what has happened? Did we both fall asleep by the fire after we ate?"

Kyle frowned. Abruptly he kicked over the thermos of tea so kindly provided for them by an unknown hand. As the rest of the dark liquid gurgled out into the ground, he nodded grimly. "There was more in that tea than we knew. It opened doors that are ordinarily closed to us. And should stay closed! Wren," Kyle questioned urgently, "How much did you see?"

Wren rubbed her forehead. "I heard the reed flute and then the glade was filled with frightened people," she began.

"You saw that?" Kyle asked incredulously. "Did you, did you see the Old One?"

"Yes. I saw everything, even when you took that strange pouch from under your shirt. Where did you get that?"

"I've always had it," Kyle confessed. "But I seldom wear it anymore. It's, it's from a part of my life that is over now ... one not worth telling you about."

Wren pressed her hand against his chest and felt the soft bulge. Slowly she withdrew the small leather bag.

"Don't open it!" Kyle cautioned sharply. "Don't even smell it!" He thrust it back under his tee shirt.

"What is it?"

"It's my Medicine Pouch. There's a powder in it that is very dangerous."

Wren sniffed her fingers. "Oh my God," she exclaimed. "It smells like the stuff the woman was....," her voice trailed off.

Kyle raised his eyebrows as Wren described her "dream".

"That wasn't a dream," he informed her with a strange look. I don't know how to explain what we just experienced ... whether it refers to the past or the future. However,"

Kyle sighed deeply, "such experiences usually presage trouble."

Wren studied Kyle's broad features in the flickering firelight. Something was emerging in the man she married and it frightened her. "How ... how do you know so much about these kind of 'visions', Kyle?"

"I've had them before," he answered somberly. Wren waited but Kyle said no more. She shivered and moved closer to the fire, away from him.

Sitting there, surrounded by the tranquil night sounds of the forest, they were tempted to doubt the reality of what they had just experienced. But when Wren shifted, trying to brush aside some pebbles, her fingers closed around something smooth and cold. It was a glass stopper from an old-fashioned medicine bottle.

"Kyle! What is all this about?"

He shook his head slowly. "I suspect Mencie could tell us but I'm not sure I want to ask *her*."

CHAPTER FIVE

Contrary to their expectations, Wren and Kyle slept deeply and dreamlessly once they finally crawled into their tent, erected beneath a large tree at the edge of the clearing. They wakened to a misty May dawn, sweet with the fragrance of wild roses and the trilling of birds. Quietly they savored their morning coffee, reveling in the sheer normality of birds feeding their young and insects flitting through grasses in the glade. Kyle disassembled their tent and deftly organized their backpacks while Wren rinsed their cups in the spring water and refilled their canteens. Then they shouldered their packs.

"Which way, Wren?" Kyle asked softly.

"Oh, Kyle," she groaned, "how can I know what we should do? After last night, I feel trapped, as if walking away now would condemn us to... to betraying someone? But frankly, I'm terrified of what we may learn if we go back to the cove." Wren rubbed her forehead and leaned against a tree. As she did so, her eye fell on the bulge under Kyle's shirt and the disk between her breasts grew hot. She touched it tentatively, as if asking a question. Kyle waited, watching her intently.

Finally, Wren threw up her hands in surrender. "We can't leave now. As you said last night, something is expected of us here. But I'll declare again," she added darkly, "I don't like this. Don't like this at all!"

Wending their way along the path back to the cove and the meeting with Jonah, Wren recalled a moment during the meal at Oma's. She turned toward Kyle. "Why were you so upset at lunch yesterday? After Jonah greeted us, you seemed... jumpy, nervous."

"I wasn't...." Kyle began defensively and then admitted, "I recognized who Jonah is. And he knew me...." Kyle snapped his mouth shut and shook his head so sharply his sweat band slipped.

Wren eyed her husband carefully. "Where did you meet him, Kyle?"

Kyle's shoulders lifted and fell. "He taught at the college I attended."

"Where you got your M.A. in Theology?" Wren dared to ask softly.

Silence greeted Wren's question. She wondered if Kyle had even heard her, absorbed as he was in some inner dialogue.

As they passed Oma's place, Mencie waved her hat at them from the porch but they did not stop. Both Wren and Kyle had a thing or two to take up with this gnome-like woman who seemed bent on engineering their lives but now was not the time. Approaching the white chapel further up the road, they studied its spare lines. Instead of a wide front entrance, there were two small doors set some distance apart.

As Wren pondered this strange feature, its purpose popped into her mind and she bristled. Kyle, observing her, chuckled.

"What? Not a fan of 'separate but equal'?" he teased.

"I've heard of congregations that separated men and women during Services but that they shouldn't even walk through the same door ...." Wren spluttered.

"Tell you what," Kyle proposed grabbing her hand. "Let's both walk through BOTH doors together and really stir up the old spirits!" Releasing tensions from the previous night, they were laughingly circling in and out when a large figure loomed out of the gloom of the interior.

"Beware what you say about the old spirits." Jonah's deep voice boomed in the empty church, disrupting their merriment and reviving their wariness.Though he wore bib overalls and a flannel shirt, there was a Presence about Jonah that faintly chided Wren's mocking spite. His bearded face radiated warmth however and Wren slowly lowered her guard. Not so Kyle. She felt him stiffen at her side, defiance playing across his usually controlled features.

Jonah observed them quietly for a few moments before addressing Kyle, his eyes grave under bushy white brows. "You remember me, don't you?" he asked.

"I do," Kyle responded curtly.

"It's been fifteen years. And you haven't resolved your problems yet, have you?" Jonah observed gently, his eyes roving over Kyle and Wren, who was studying her husband anxiously.

"What problems is he talking about, Kyle?"

Kyle shrugged and turned away to stare out the church window at the cemetery on the hillside. Wren sensed his turmoil and her apprehensions revived. Jonah, she suspected, posed a threat to her life with Kyle, one connected to parts of her husband's past that Kyle had deliberately hidden from her. She put her hand on Kyle's arm and was dismayed by his lack of response. He was far away from her in a place where she could not reach him.

"Why don't we sit outside in the sunshine?" Jonah suggested. They clattered out of the echoing chapel and threaded their way among the gravestones to a dip in the grassy slope. Wren considered excusing herself so Jonah and Kyle could talk more freely but Jonah forestalled her even as the thought formed in her mind. "Wren, stay. We need you," he rumbled and chuckled at her start of surprise. She found this business of having her mind read not a little disturbing.

For a few minutes no one spoke as they sat in the mild May sunlight, listening to the birds and other, less audible voices that seemed to come from within themselves and (Wren shivered) from the cold graves around them.

Finally, Jonah began softly, "You're surprised, Kyle, to discover ol' Jonah here when you knew me as Dr. John Augburn?

But I am truly Jonah and my shipmates were right to toss me overboard when they did. I was running away from God then and nearly betrayed him." He paused, smiling sadly.

"You know what it means to be traveling in the belly of paradox, Kyle?"

Kyle looked up but said nothing.

"It means you fall into the hands of the Living God," Jonah continued. "A fearful thing, that! The guts of a whale are definitely preferable! Let me explain," he raised his hand to silence the questions forming on Kyle's lips.

"As you know, I was teaching Scripture as if there were no church tradition. A major 'no-no' in our circles! To my mind, two thousand years of 'interpretation' and tradition had distorted the Gospel message, betraying rather than fulfilling it. An observation by G.K. Chesterton captures my feelings neatly: 'Christianity has not been tried and found wanting; it has yet to be tried.'"

Kyle interrupted, "I can't forget the day you threw that quote down like a gauntlet before us students, daring us to pick it up. You declared that if there are still so many people looking for the Messiah it is because there is little evidence among us "Christians" that he has come. I left class that day very angry with you and it merged with my anger that truths written on my soul had to be suppressed because they didn't harmonize with 'revelation.' If what you said was true, the

The White Church

'religion' for which I had sacrificed my heritage was itself a betrayal ... and what a fool that made me! I feared you, I hated you, you and the anger you were unleashing within me."

"So did others!" Jonah boomed. "I was impatient back then. Like Jonah, I did not want the 'great city, Nineveh' to be converted and live. Rather I wanted the whole structure to be destroyed, preferably in my lifetime, and I wanted to be among those calling down the fire and brimstone."

Wren looked at the huge man before her and could vividly imagine him doing precisely that. "You don't feel that way now?" she ventured.

She was surprised to see tears mist Jonah's deep blue eyes.

"It is so easy to be *against* something in the name of being *for* Someone." he observed wryly. "I was a blind leader of the blind... may God have mercy on me. And He has, He has," he marveled softly.

"My views were correctly perceived as dangerous by persons who blindly embraced and defended the Faith as they knew it. But the ideas were even more dangerous to those of us who accepted them; who mistook hatred for zeal; flames of destruction for the purifying fire; darkness for light. And I myself was chief among these latter."

Kyle beat a balled fist against the ground. "So why did you just walk away, Dr. John? Without a word of explanation or apology? We were left with no answers to unbearable questions; questions that shattered the whole structure of our belief system and left us with only scattered pieces of a puzzle that had no frame- work."

Jonah sighed. "I did worse than that, son. I left you without all the pieces. No way could you (or any of us) construct a whole picture with so few fragments. Just as I was about to hammer my own "Doctrine of Destruction" on the cathedral door, as it were, I was summoned back here."

"How was that?" Kyle frowned, wondering yet again

what this cove was really about.

"My folks were from here originally. They moved out even before the trains stopped running and never came back. However, they spoke so often of their home place in the Smokies that it lived on within me. One night as I was pounding away at my computer in a frenzy, the screen went blank. So did my mind. And I heard something like a Voice that reverberated throughout my whole being. 'Return! Return!'"

Kyle and Wren nodded in agreement. "We felt that coming in - like we were being called back!"

"I was stunned," Jonah continued. "I looked at that dead computer screen and it was a mirror where I saw the reflection of my soul...horrible. Do you believe that what we worship is written on our faces? And what we are worshipping, we are becoming?" He paused and drew in a shuddering breath.

"I was becoming exactly what I was trying to destroy! My mind was so dominated with rage over the betrayal of Jesus' message (as I perceived it), that I had failed to see what a traitor to it, to Him, I was becoming. I was far closer to being a Judas than a merely ludicrous Jonah at that moment! I had to leave ... before I used you and others for an end that would have twisted you as thoroughly as it was distorting me."

Jonah continued, anguish throbbing in his voice. "So I tried to find my way back here. It isn't easy when you don't know the way. I must've spent two weeks wandering alone through these mountains. My camp supplies were used up and my strength just about gone when one night a fog rolled in so thick that I literally could not see my hand before my face. I stumbled and fell down a ravine, crashing through brambles and bouncing off rocks until I landed in a laurel break so tangled I was entrapped. I was as imprisoned bodily as I was spiritually. Only then, when I couldn't do a thing to help myself, help came."

Wren had an intuitive vision of a floppy gray hat and so was not surprised when Jonah said humbly. "Mencie found me." Wren could clearly picture that gnome-like little figure peering through the twisted laurel and ordering the disoriented professor: "Follow me, if you please."

"And you followed her, of course," Wren murmured.

"What else?" Jonah responded dryly.

Kyle broke the silence that momentarily overtook them. "What is this place? It is the most ... most eerie place I've ever been. These people shouldn't be here. What I've seen of their life makes no sense. But, but it is so good," Kyle struggled. "And true? Yes, like homemade bread is true ... made from genuine stuff. But... it's also dangerous, isn't it? Like, well, like too much sanity, perhaps. You can lose yourself, at least the self you think you are. So, what then is real?" He shook his head.

'Those were my questions exactly, when I first met the Elders. And, to some extent, they are still my questions." Jonah responded. 'This place is an enigma. It is the most defenseless and simple and yet, protected place I've ever known. Consider the Power that is concentrated here ...."

"Power?" Kyle and Wren echoed together.

Jonah made no attempt to answer them. He just looked deep into their eyes and all the experiences they had had in the past twenty-four hours rushed in on them. Just as they were about to ask Jonah about the Borderlands, Mencie called out from the road, "Jonah, there's a message for you at the house. Oma got it this morning."

"Umph, this could be urgent," Jonah muttered to himself as he rose quickly to his feet. "Sorry to leave you like this but there will be another time ...." and he strode briskly toward the road.

"Not again!" Kyle growled, kicking the earth so that pebbles flew. Wren backed off, fearful of what was happening in the man she had married, and began to wander among the gravestones. Like most cemeteries it was a peaceful place and she began to distract herself by reading names and dates inscribed on the weathered stones. Soon Kyle joined her and they vied with one another, trying to find the earliest dates. Kyle found one from 1862, just as the civil war was beginning to turn Blackburne County into a land of hunted men and boys.

Wren had read that the mountain folk didn't care about either the Union or the Confederacy. All they wanted was for the government to stay far away. Benign neglect by Washington inclined the mountaineers to side with the Union. But North Carolina, in voting to secede, had pledged its men to fight under the Confederate flag. Periodic raids to round up recruits for the South angered many a mountain family and soon, in addition to mountain dew, able-bodied men were being smuggled through the passes to Kentucky and the Union forces.

Kyle wondered if the folk of Lovada Branch had been involved in this dangerous traffic. He doubted that the Lovada men would have fought for either side. For one thing the only graves of young men buried during the war years were those over around the Bentley place. Had some sort of raid or betrayal taken place there?

Wren was examining some crumbling bits of granite set upright in the ground with only a few rough scratches still visible on them. She made out a date -1784. She'd no idea that there were settlers in this area that early. Tripping over a stump, Wren caught at the nearest object, a block of rough cement.

"Kyle, come over here," she called out. When he arrived, Wren was puzzling over the strange lettering on the stone. "What language is this?"

Squatting before the crudely shaped marker, Kyle traced the scratches. Some of them reminded him of the Hebrew

he had studied in school; or the Cyrillic alphabet. "Here? In this Cove?

Wren asked if it could be the written form of Cherokee. One of their chiefs, Tecumseh, had developed an alphabet for his people - the first such for a Native American people. Had some Cherokee died in The Cove and been buried here? The grave marker itself was obviously handmade by someone unskilled in the craft. The letters, instead of being incised into the cement, were actually raised.

Wren ran her fingers thoughtfully over the uneven letters. They looked like the printing of someone with dyslexia. Letters were backwards.... "Kyle! Where is my pack? Did we leave our stuff at the church door?" Even as she spoke, Wren rushed toward the chapel and fished through her toiletries. Seizing her mirror, she scurried back to the grave.

Kyle had caught on and before Wren could say a word, he took the mirror and told her to stand behind the small stone where she could see its reflection in the glass. Wren stooped down and squinted at the small image in Kyle's hand.

"It reads 'Winnie Lovada'!" Wren gasped, "... my ... my great Mamaw." Suddenly she tripped and fell against the fragile headstone which tilted sideways taking Wren with it. A gash of cold, black earth opened under her and she felt again the wraith-like sensation of her "nightmare" from the previous evening.

A voice resounded in her ears: "Don't fight so, girl. I won't hurt you. I love you." A woman moaned and Wren recognized the despairing voice from her earlier vision. A rhythmic ebb and flow of waters shushed in her ears. Briefly, Wren felt the warm security of the womb enveloping her. But the body that held her thrashed in anguish. "No, no," the woman muttered and the pulse beat surrounding Wren grew erratic.

Once again, the woman felt herself being forced down, down and smothered by a heavy, grasping weight. Her horror and helplessness to prevent what was happening wrought a curious disengagement from the body lying on the floor. From a distance she watched the two writhing figures. Whatever was happening could not reach her here.

Impressions flooded Wren's unconscious, an awareness of something so horrifying her mind refused to accept it. Profound depression accompanied by a certainty that she should never have been, overwhelmed Wren.

From somewhere far off, Wren heard Kyle's anxious voice calling out to her. She flung herself toward it. A firm hand seized her shoulder. She grabbed it tightly and suddenly, sweet May sunlight warmed her face. Slowly she opened her eyes and looked up into Kyle's worried face.

"Wren. Wren. I'm right here! What happened? Are you all right?" he whispered anxiously.

She shook her head. "Yes, I mean no. I don't know... I don't know if I've ever been alright." She stared up at Kyle in confusion.

"Wren, what do you mean ... not alright?" Kyle asked. "Better not to have been born." muttered Wren heavily. In response to Kyle's troubled look, she added, "I don't know why I feel this way.... but part of me has always felt I was no good, no, not good at all." Wren shuddered as Kyle folded her in his arms and kissed her reddish curls.

"I want to help you, Wren," he murmured. "Can you tell me anything at all about this?"

Wren was silent for so long, Kyle began to fear she was going to insist on handling this alone. His every instinct shouted that if she tried, it would prove a trap.

Something of his fear communicated itself to Wren and warred with forces trying to control her. Her lips and tongue felt stiff as if a hand were pressed hard against her mouth. She realized it was her own. Slowly Wren allowed the

57

warmth and insistence of Kyle's love to overcome the terror holding her captive.

Maybe there was a way to escape from under the crushing weight she felt. Licking her lips and struggling against a force that sought to restrain her, Wren began. "You, you remember what, what I told you about my "vision" last night? This was more of it ... and it is real! The unborn child I saw then - it was me but it shouldn't have been. I shouldn't have been there. Do you understand?"

Kyle frowned and shook his head but silently urged her on. Wren squeezed her eyes shut and whispered, "It has something to do with blood, bad blood... my blood." Wren nodded, then continued slowly.

"That girl, the one I saw, didn't want to let me happen... and that refusal deep inside allowed her to reach out for help. Just now, she reached me. I think she is living in me... but," Wren's voice grew hoarse, "she's dead, Kyle. Am I doomed, too?"

As Kyle listened, some deep Cherokee knowing stirred him. Briefly, he glimpsed again the Ancient One who had returned the leather pouch to him, the pouch that contained the hallucinogenic powders. The Old One had known that Kyle would have need for it. Foreboding weighed heavily on his spirit, further entangling the emotions aroused by today's meeting with Jonah.

Kyle rocked Wren slowly and whispered, "There may be a way out of this, dear, but it could be risky."

Suddenly Wren slipped out of Kyle's grasp. "I don't want to involve you in this! It is my burden alone." She brushed frantically at her jeans and boots, trying to remove a stain only she could perceive.

"Wren," Kyle responded anxiously, "Don't push me out. There's love here too, as well as darkness."

"I wish I were sure of that," Wren responded morosely.

"Listen up, girl!" a voice briskly commanded. Wren and

Kyle jumped, startled to see Mencie advancing toward them. Her gray hat drooped and her poncho flapped, creating the impression of a walking tent. She looked at them, golden eyes, wise and sad. "Follow me if you please." she ordered.

CHAPTER SIX

Wren shot Kyle a vexed glance and shrugged resignedly. They reclaimed their gear and hurried along behind Mencie who was trotting briskly toward a path they had not noticed. She was singing softly, a haunting variation of "Were you there?" The words seized Wren's soul so powerfully that it didn't register when she and Kyle actually began singing along. Mantra-like, the chanting seemed to rinse her eyes, cleanse her vision. The woods around her seemed to shine with unusual freshness. Her fears abated; her grief was assuaged and her anger was tempered ... for the moment at least.

Kyle, too, seemed to be affected by the potent words. Wren noted a visionary light in his face that awed her. Glancing back, Mencie nodded, as if satisfied. Then she urged them on, "You'ns need to meet Haidia and Bewley. They're Lore-Keepers for the Cove." A well-worn path was leading them toward a small cabin of weathered wood that blended into the shadows of the great trees surrounding it.

Mencie gestured toward some towering evergreens and stopped. "The guardian pines," she murmured, and bowed briefly before stepping into the glade beyond them. Nestled in the shadows, Kyle and Wren discerned the contours of a house that defied description. It was a jumble of roof angles and oddly shaped windows that somehow fit harmoniously into the slope of the hollow cradling it.

"Haidia? Bewley?" Mencie called out. "You'ns to home?"

The ringing of an axe ceased abruptly and a smiling man limped around the corner of the house, a stray beam of sunlight brightening his halo of white hair. Movement on the screened-in porch caught Wren's attention. An angular woman, iron-gray braids wrapped around her head, quickly set down a pan of strawberries she had been hulling.

"You'ns come on in." Haidia invited, swinging open the screen door. Colorful rag rugs lay among cane-bottom chairs, a swing and a rocker, the latter occupied by a magnificent gray cat that regarded them with regal disdain.

"Meet The Dean," Haidia said and ritually presented first Wren's and then Kyle's hand to be sniffed. Apparently satisfied, "The Dean" rose, stretched, and sauntered out the door Mencie held open for him. Bewley ascended the three steps slowly, dragging a twisted leg.

"You'ns Winnie Lovada and Kyle, ain't ya? See'd ya last evenin' in the meader when the kids come in," Bewley observed.

"Set yourselves down," Haidia urged and stepped through the inner door, returning shortly with glasses of iced tea and large oatmeal cookies heaped on a tray. "We was 'spectin' ya. You'ns must have lots of questions 'bout now. Mencie said she'd bring you 'round.'"

"That was good of her," Wren commented wryly and winced as Kyle pinched her elbow. Mencie seated herself in the vacated rocker, still humming softly. An inexplicable contentment settled over Kyle and Wren as they sipped their tea on this quiet porch, a breeze soughing through hemlocks and white pines. Hummingbirds buzzed and darted about a feeder, the fierce defense of their territory in marked contrast to the peace that pervaded this holler.

Searching for an innocuous way to open the conversation, Kyle observed, "You two must know a lot of stories about Lovada Branch." He and Wren swayed slowly on the swing.

"Reckon we do," Bewley admitted. "What you want to hear about first?"

Kyle sensed they were in the presence of a master storyteller and grinned in anticipation. "Tell us how this cove was settled. Who first came here? What was the community like? We came across some intriguing hints in the cemetery. What happened to folks after the trains stopped running?"

Haidia chuckled as Bewley put up his hand. "Whoa, young man. You're talkin' more'n two hunderd years of livin', lovin', fightin' and dyin'. Ah cain't give it all to ya in one settin'. Ah'll rough out a bit of the story and we can fill in the details about folks later on."

Bewley took a long draft of his iced tea, wiped the back of his hand across his mouth and tilted his chair back. "Les' see now. Folks began follerin' a trace along the Forever River back in the 1740's. On their way to Tennessee, some of 'em turned off and walked up this here bold branch tumbling down out of the Unaka Mountains.

"Didn't fancy goin' along with ever'body else," Haidia put in. "They was mostly Scots-Irish, you see," she added, as if this explained it.

Bewley picked up. "Twas all virgin land in those days, covered with trees ... walnuts eight feet across; tulip poplars runnin' up to twelve. They say one of the first families in The Cove lived in a holler tree their first summer."

"Probably some of the Cutshall's," interjected Haidia. "They was here in the valley early on."

"I saw that name in the cemetery!" exclaimed Wren.

"So you did, honey," Haidia observed. "One of 'em is your great-great-Mamaw. They's good folk, never mind what...."

Bewley stepped in smoothly, "Talkin' about beginnin's,

we'd best tell about the Cherokee. They'd lived here for hunderds of years before airy a white man heard of these mountains. It was a summer huntin' ground for'em."

Kyle's eyes met Bewley's who held his gaze and nodded. "Yep, they passed through here a lot. Too far off for a permanent town, I guess, and that's what helped save them in the end. Some of 'em anyway. These Cherokee weren't no trouble to folks who settled The Cove so they traded with them, learned a lot from 'em about these mountains. Even when the French stirred up the Cherokee nation against the English in the 1750's, it didn't cause folks here no worry. Fact is, when the Governor of North Carolina sent Hugh Waddell and the army to crush the Cherokee, their chiefs sent some of their women and children to this Cove for safekeepin'."

Bewley gave Kyle a speculative look. "You might know some- thin' about this, son, if you know your own blood. Not all of the Cherokee knew the secret trails in and out of here. They'd be posted and when the warriors smuggled some of their old folks and children up here, the sentinels would find'em and guid'em in."

Involuntarily, Kyle's hand touched the bulge under his shirt where the leather pouch hung like a weight about his neck. Mencie gave Bewley and Haidia a knowing glance and they nodded respectfully toward Kyle. He stirred uneasily, rubbing a sweaty palm along his jeans. Wren frowned as she grew more and more perplexed by Kyle's behavior.

Bewley just kept talking. "After the so-called peace treaty of 1761, when most of the Cherokee nation were pretty much beat down, those hid here pledged never to harm our folk. And they din't neither! Some of the Indian fighters suspicioned that bands of Cherokee were hidin' out here but the folks in The Cove had no mind to mention it to army scouts that passed through here lookin' for'em." He chuckled. "Even back then, no one here abouts had any use for what gov'mints wanted."

"Welp, when it was safe, the Indians went on down into Georgia where livin' was a bit easier for 'em and folk here jist carried on. We had our own mill and church and school for the young'uns. We farmed the flat land and run cattle on the slopes. There was a smithy and wagon-maker and cobbler. What we couldn't make ourselves, we bartered for coffee, sugar and salt and some pretties for the girls."

Bewley grinned over at Haidia.

"You want to know what we bartered with?" she picked up. "It's a long narrow trail out of here, too rough for wagons, so we had to use pack mules and such. It was a sight easier to pack out corn in liquid form than in bushel bags. We grew some good leaf for 'bacca, too and that fetched a high price in Greenville or Lashton. Most ever' family put in some for a cash crop."

Bewley continued, "When secession happened, no one around here much cared. We didn't think of ourselves as livin' in North Carolina that went Confederate nor in Tennessee neither. Fact is, we still don't. Bet you didn't find Lovada Cove on either map."

Wren shook her head. "We didn't. I came across a map of the old state of Franklin that showed Lovada Branch where Loverly Branch runs today. Only a couple of older folks were willing to talk to us about Lovada Cove. Nobody said a word about anyone still living back here. Do they not know?"

"Oh, they know right well, honey," Haidia said. "But it's agin their loyalty to say anythin' ... 'lessen they know for sure they're talkin' to someone what belongs back here. That's why Miss Althea and ole Gaither told you as much as they did."

Wren's eye's widened. "How did you know they were the ones we talked with? And how would they know whether we were meant to find The Cove? We didn't know it ourselves!"

"Din't you, honey? Then why was ya searchin'? You was lookin' to come home and they know'd you had a right to find yore way back to your home place.It's written all over you for those what can see."

"For those who can see," Kyle repeated slowly. "That's like something," he nodded toward Mencie, "you said ... you told us that only those come here who are 'Sent' or 'Summoned.' Have you got folks out there who do the 'Sending'? Something like the Cherokee sentinels?"

Bewley drawled, "Hit ain't so simple as all that but yore onto somethin'." He looked a question at Mencie who shook her head. "Guess you'll be findin' out more 'bout that later on." He paused and then resumed, "Now durin' the war, The Cove wasn't sendin' its men out to fight on either side. By then, our church was teachin' us about a different W a y from hatin' and killin'. But occasionally, when our people were out in the Borderlands they'd meet up with patrols lookin' for fightin' men for one side or the other. Weren't hard to avoid'em as a rule. What was harder was when we come upon some bunch of fool-heads lookin' to get away from one army by jinin' up with another."

Bewley smiled sadly. "They'd be lost and hungry,like as not, so we'd feed'm and send'm safely on their way. Once only, a bunch of ours got jumped and captured. The sergeant who got'em didn't have much control of his own men, I guess. Instead of takin'em back to the camp like they should 'a had, they peeled off a bunch and took'em into the woods and shot'em there. Most of em were from one family that had gone out deer huntin'."

"They was the Bentleys, mostly," Haidia chimed in. "Some of em was still kids, fourteen, sixteen years old. Others of em were past fightin' age, in their forties, even."

Kyle recalled the tumbled headstones in the overgrown

65

cemetery near the Bentley place but before he could say anything, Haidia nodded, "Yep, that's them. Others of ours found their bodies and buried them. What puzzled folks was why they got caught in the first place? But strange things happen out there in the Borderlands from time to time."

Wren stirred uneasily but before she could formulate her thoughts, Mencie broke in.

"Tell'em about what happened after the trains stopped comin' in, Bewley," she prompted.

"Well, yeh," he started and tugged on his ear. "Les' see now, the first tracks got laid along the Forever River through these parts after the War but it wasn't until 1884, when the Southern Railroad Company bought up the entire line, did they run a spur up along Lovada Branch. They was after the timber, you know, but folks in The Cove found it mighty convenient for sendin' out their 'bacca and steers and sich-like. After a while, the young'uns started shippin' out, too. Lots of the farms jest went back to wild then."

"Like the Bentley place?" Wren interjected.

"No. That'n was abandoned later," Haidia began. But before she could continue, Bewley broke in on her.

"Like ah said, we cain't tell all the stories at this one settin', Haidia. Let that'n rest fer a bit. What ah want to tell now is about how those who left returned tellin' us that the world out there was mighty different from here in The Cove." He glanced at Mencie again and she nodded.

"Ah said we had our own church. But when we built it we had no preacher fer it and no one could figure out how to git one to come back in here. Ever' Sunday someone would ring the bell and we would all gather and sit there in the church, jest thinkin' and prayin' about it. Then one time it happened that Luther Jake Ammons got up to read from the big bible that was open on the pulpit. The way my Granny tole it, it was spring so they was readin' about the resurrection and all. Well, ole Luther, he's readin' aloud and ever'body's concentratin' and it gets real quiet. He's readin' about the women goin' weepin' to the tomb and how sudden-like, they see this stranger who asks, "Why seek ye the living one among the dead? He is not here. He has been raised up."

"And that's when lil' Lori Bell spoke up," broke in Haidia. "She was all of five years, I guess. And she jest asked so simple: 'Well, if He ain't dead, where is He?' No one said anythin' fer a bit. Seems like somethin' was goin' on and no one knew what to say."

"Suddenly Ada Sue stood up and commenced lookin' around at ever'body," Bewley explained. "Ada was my granny's cousin and they was sittin' next to one another. Ada jest whispered real quiet- like but everybody heard her. 'Ah do believe He's walkin' here among us.' And ever'body knew what she said was true. No point in lookin' among the dead. He was there among them in that church house."

"Granny said it was the strangest thing. Folks began lookin' at one another with the question, 'Are you him? Or is he Uncle Sibbald over there in the corner?' This went on fer a bit until Luther Jake nearly dropped the Book when his grandson run up to him with eyes big as saucers and asked, 'Papaw, be you Jesus?'

Ole' Luther'd been watchin' ever'body lookin' at ever'body else wonderin' if he or she was the Living One. 'Twas likely someone among them was Him but did it really matter knowin' which one? Granny said she was wonderin' about Ada Sue and was goin' to test her by touchin' her dress when Ada turned 'round to Granny and said real soft, 'Laura? Be you the one?"

"Well, right about then someone commenced singing, 'Are you here at his risin' from the dead? Are you here at his risin' from the dead? Oh, how it's causin' me to tremble, tremble, tremble. Are you here at his risin' from the dead?' They was all pretty good at singing and it wasn't long before

67

they was all harmonizin' and makin' up new verses and all."

"Lori Bell, the little'un I told ya 'bout," chimed in Haidia, "Why she started in on singin' 'Yes, ah'm here at his risin' from the dead.' And soon ever'body was jest a cryin' and carryin' on so happy-like." Haidia wiped her eyes on the corner of her apron.

Kyle and Wren were holding hands, shivers racing through them. They had recognized the chant Mencie had sung along their way here. Then Haidia raised up the ice tea pitcher and refilled their glasses. As Kyle told Wren later, he half feared Haidia would suddenly vanish from their sight but instead she just settled stiffly back onto her chair. The Dean was back in the rocker, his paws curled under him.

Wren turned to Kyle and whispered, "My heart is just about on fire. What is happening here?"

Kyle responded slowly. "My heart is burning, too. Maybe He truly is here among us today? We may never know exactly what happened in that church a few generations back but can we deny what we're feeling after Bewley opened that Scripture reading for us?"

Haidia observed this quiet interchange with keen interest. A gentle smile softened her features. She prodded Bewley, "Well, go on. That ain't the end of our story."

"No, Haidia, it sure ain't!" Bewley agreed. "Hit's more like the beginnin'. There was a sweet anointin' that morning that has touched ever'one of us. Those who left took the message with them."

"You mean, folks went out telling people that the Messiah was living back here in Lovada Cove?" Kyle asked.

"No, sir, they did not! But having grow'd up with Him at hand, they went out livin' the message."

"It wouldn't be all that easy," Wren commented softly.

"Nope, it ain't. Bein' lovin' and acceptin' and not judgin' other folks jist never come easy to no one, I guess," Haidia observed. "But because we was mostly poor and didn't count for nothin' out there, no one really paid us much mind."

"Except for those who was really hurtin' or in need of a friend or just plain huntin' for somethin' more," interjected Bewley. 'They was folks who found this kind of livin' and lovin' the answer to whatever pain life had dealt them. Some even found their way here to The Cove."

'They was the ones who went through the Trial," Haidia added cryptically.

'Trial?" Wren asked anxiously.

Haidia and Bewley studied the younger couple, compassion mellowing their aged features. "There be a Trial for ever'one who comes. Some pass; some don't," Bewley drawled softly.

"Even for the people who are born and raised here?" Wren persisted.

"Especially for them," Haidia murmured. "That's why we all leave before we're grow'd up. No one can jest hang in here without payin'." She patted Bewley's twisted leg.

Kyle opened his mouth to ask more but thought better of it. Why inquire about something he had been running from all his life? Maybe it was time to yield to Wren's wish and leave while they were still able, and return to a life they were familiar with. Deep within however, he feared it might already be too late.

Wren was pushing their swing with unnecessary vigor, her slim hands twisting in her lap. She wasn't any more at ease than Kyle. She'd sought healing on this journey, not fresh wounds.

Bewley and Haidia were silent for a while, as if awaiting a cue about how to proceed. Finally, Bewley sighed, 'Those folks who make it back here stay until they're ready and then leave agin. No one keeps track but now and again, we hear there be another Cove Community happenin' somewhere and we're glad fer'em."

"Are there many such?" Kyle asked intently.

"Reckon there are," Bewley mused. "More than we know. It got hard for folks to get in and out of here after the mudslide washed out the train tracks in the '20's. They wasn't replaced 'cause all this became federal parkland along about then and ever'body was expected to move out."

"Like over in Cades Cove?" Wren queried, worry edging her voice. "No one lives there anymore. How come you are still here?"

"Well, it was jist one of those things." Bewley drawled with a sly wink. "The park rangers come in here lookin' to tell us to leave and ... well, they jist never found us." Wren and Kyle exchanged a look of bewilderment but Bewley sat silent, his words sinking in.

Finally, Wren and Kyle spluttered together, "Never found you? Never found a whole community of people living and farming and ... and ...." Wren wrinkled her brow in disbelief.

"I suppose it sounds a might strange," Haidia agreed. "But we have our ways, don't you know."

"No, we don't know," Kyle broke in roughly.

"You may get a chance to find out soon enough," Bewley predicted ominously. "There's a meetin' of the guardians and faith-keepers tonight at the church before the young folk leave. Kyle, Winnie Lovada, we'll be expectin' you there."

"Guardians? Faith-keepers?" Kyle echoed. "Just what are you talking about?" He slammed his hand on his knee impatiently. "I'm fed up with all this, this mystery. It's just too much."

He looked around for Mencie but didn't see her. Only the gray eminence of The Dean regarded him steadily from the rocker where Mencie had been sitting. He felt the hairs on the back of his neck rising. Wren's gaze had followed Kyle's and she slipped a cold hand into his.

Haidia got up stiffly and patted the thin gray braids twisted around her head. "We'd be mighty proud to have you to dinner but Zettie Lovada sent over to invite you back to her place. I reckon you'll want to spend as much time as you kin with your Mamaw, Winnie, and I don't blame you none. So you two jest git yourselves on over there and know we don't take no hurt from it. Here, take these strawberries along with you. If you'ns are lucky, Zettie will have stirred up a batch of her biscuits."

Before Wren could utter a word, she and Kyle were ushered down the porch steps with directions from Bewley about taking the right-hand fork back up the trail. Shrugging into their gear, Kyle and Wren started up the path that led through the guardian pines. They were passing under the thick boughs when a sharp meow brought them up short. The Dean blocked their way.

"How did he get here?" grumbled Wren.

Kyle studied his aggressive stance. "He's deliberately blocking the path. I wonder what he wants?"

A soft breeze stirred through the branches and reminded them of Mencie's bow as they approached Haidia and Bewley's.

"This is crazy," muttered Wren as she and Kyle bowed awkwardly toward the tall shapely pines that reminded them of veiled matrons watching over the little house in the hollow. Kyle's expression was thoughtful.

"I wonder if my ancestors honored any of the trees in this cove," he mused. "According to Bewley, there must have been some magnificent specimens here before timbering stripped the slopes." He laid a hand on the ridged bark of the nearest tree and thrilled to feel its stretch and stress as a gust of wind tossed the branches near its top.

"I guess we can move on now," Wren broke in. "The Dean is satisfied." She eyed the gray cat now parading down the path ahead of them, fluffy tail erect and purpose in its trot.

71

"A cat with a mission," commented Kyle.

"This is growing more and more bizarre," Wren said in hushed tones. Both of them recalled following another gray figure up this same path. At a fork in the path, The Dean stopped and pointed with his nose toward the right. "Why do I feel we are being shepherded around this cove?" Wren inquired of no one in particular.

"Meu-ar", The Dean announced before turning back down the trail.

"Wha-a-t?" Wren gasped as she watched the departing tail. "This is just too much. First we are bowing to trees, now we are conversing with cats! Why...."

Kyle laid his hand gently across her mouth. "Don't ask," he begged, "I'm afraid of the answer! It will only raise a dozen more questions and we've run across more mystery in the past twenty-four hours than I want to deal with as is!"

The Dean

67

CHAPTER SEVEN

Wren agreed without too much hesitation and they turned up the right fork in silence. Their path bordered a stream that gurgled around mossy stones and foamed over a small falls. The rushing water was occasionally obscured by thick stands of laurel on its banks, some still sprinkled with the last of its pale blooms.

The woodland around them echoed with bird songs, many of which Kyle recognized. A few melodies were unfamiliar, however, and he wondered if some threatened species had found sanctuary in this cove as had, he reflected, some unusual human types as well. Kyle's father had left these mountains after marrying a woman he had met while studying in Chapel Hill. But he had passed on his woods lore and family traditions to his sons during annual visits with relatives who still lived on the Qualla Boundary of the Cherokee.

Kyle felt at home on this woodland path and allowed himself to relax amid the sounds and smells and sights of the living forest. One birdsong, though, distracted his reverie. He heard it close by and being answered further away. There was something vaguely wrong about the call. Pausing, he tried to identify why it disturbed him. When it came again and was answered from deeper in the woods, his perplexity increased. Catching up with Wren, he asked if she had also heard the sharp, clear whistles.

"They're just cardinals, aren't they? Common enough around here."

Kyle ran his fingers through the thick silvery hair dangling over his forehead. "Yes, they are native to these parts but ... they only whistle like that during the winter months. This time of year they sing a different song for their mates and young. Either they are issuing a warning about something distressing them or...."

"Or what?" Wren broke in, worried by Kyle's concern.

"Or it isn't birds we're hearing."

"Not birds? You mean some folks are doing birdcalls? Like the boys howling like red wolves at midday? Sounds like another harmless game, then."

"Yeah, I guess that's it," Kyle conceded reluctantly, adding under his breath. "But they're too good for mere fun."

They reached a small ford where stepping stones had been conveniently placed. "Beware of water snakes, oh, Sloshing Bird," Kyle teased and Wren shook her walking staff at him.

"Thanks! I needed to hear that," she retorted, with a grin. Nevertheless she studied the stones and gravelly bottom carefully before following Kyle across. On the further side, they found a fallen log by the path and with wordless agreement settled down on it. Wren leaned her head against Kyle's shoulder as he put his arm around her. Pensively, she kicked at the kettle of strawberries they were taking to Zettie Lovada.

"How do you feel about seeing Zettie again?" Kyle ventured.

"All in a turmoil," Wren confessed. "On the one hand, I find her so comforting, like I always imagined a Granny

75

would be. On the other hand, her ways disturb me. She sees the world differently than I do. How can she expect me to forgive Della?" Wren asked testily, emotion snagging her voice.

Kyle rubbed her shoulders but said nothing.

"Being here in this cove, where there is so much peace, brings out all the old questions, the old fears, the old hurts." Her shoulders sagged. "I hate admitting this but I'm eaten up with a desire to make my birthmother hurt as much as she hurt me."

"That's no small grief," Kyle offered sympathetically.

"It's getting harder to stay angry, though," Wren added slowly. "Why is that? I'm afraid that if we stay here much longer, I may lose it altogether, or be changed in ways I don't want... or understand."

Kyle stared off among the trees, somber and silent for a time. Finally he observed, "We'll both be changed ... if we survive the test."

"You mean the Trial Bewley and Haidia talked about?" Wren asked with a frown.

"Whether we know it or not, I suspect we're being sent on what my people call a Quest. It's not something you embark on lightly. And not something you return from unchanged." Softly Kyle added, "It's what I've been running from all my life."

Wren jerked around and studied Kyle's drawn features. "Are you afraid, too?" She searched his eyes anxiously.

"Much afraid," Kyle whispered. 'The testing I foresee could tear us limb from limb."

"Can it tear us apart?" Wren asked with a tremor.

"I pray not," Kyle said hoarsely. "But then, who would listen to my prayers?"

Wren shivered and involuntarily shifted away from Kyle's embrace. He let her go, lost in his own concerns. They heard the warning whistle of the cardinals again. One seemed closer than before and Kyle half-turned on the log, trying to glimpse movement in the thick green foliage surrounding them.

A sound like a soft wind approaching filled the woods and before they knew it, the leaves around them began to dip and flip from fat raindrops falling through the canopy above them.

"We'd better move on," Kyle said as they hastily dug ponchos from their packs. Donning wide-brimmed hats, they traipsed up the winding path, the music of the rain and the incense of woodsy aromas filling them with a pleasant sense of oneness with the wild world surrounding them. Before long, they crossed a footbridge into the grassy yard behind Zettie's little house. Dodging around the beehives set at the edge of the grass, they glimpsed the tiny, white-haired lady rushing to take in some nearly dry laundry. Wren scurried over to help.

Hastily they unclipped towels and sheets flapping on the lines and bundled them into a basket to fold later. Kyle set the kettle of strawberries on the back porch and ran to help them with the last items just as a roll of thunder announced the drizzle was about to become a downpour. Breathlessly Wren and Kyle rushed the clothesbasket under the sheltering porch roof with Zettie following, dropping the last of the clothespins into her apron pocket.

The heavens opened as Zettie pulled back the screen door to admit Kyle and Wren to her kitchen. Once inside, the roar of rain beating down on the tin roof drowned out any attempt at casual conversation. Zettie indicated they should take the clothesbasket into the bedroom opening off the kitchen while she pulled a teakettle over to a hotter spot on the wood stove. Wren and Kyle welcomed the steaming mugs of tea for the storm created a sudden drop in temperature. Sipping gratefully they gathered with Zettie at

Karen Karper Fredette

a table spread with red gingham.

The storm's fury abated as quickly as it had arisen and the deafening roar on the roof diminished. Helping her Granny with these homely chores had relaxed Wren's worries about being with Zettie Lovada again and soon they were chatting easily with Kyle chiming in from time to time. Zettie proudly described her other grandchildren.

"My two boys still live in Blackburne County. Locke kep' on with the 'bacca farming - never married. Porter, he went on to college, the first young'n from the Branch to do so. Clyde and me 'bout bust with pride when we saw him get his diploma. Now he's principal of the high school. Imagine that!" Zettie nodded in satisfaction.

"He gave me and Clyde three gran' babies," Zettie informed them proudly.

"Do they ever come back to see you?" Wren asked.

"Whenever they kin," Zettie acknowledged. "Fact is, Ah'm s'pectin' the boys to turn up tonight for the meetin'. Most of the younger generation are too busy to get back here often but they know the way and always come when needed." Her eyes rested fondly on Wren.

"Seems like it's you we need now, child," she added softly and Wren felt tears start to her eyes, blurring her vision of the large, plain kitchen with its shelves covered with flowered curtains and an old wringer-washer in the corner. The aroma of wood smoke, just-baked biscuits and fresh laundry mingled on the air. Wren breathed deeply and leaned back in her chair, a faint smile softening her features.

"My, you are the image of Della," Zettie marveled, "same hair and coloring, same eyes and build. 'Course I never saw her at your age but I always tried to picture what she'd look like as the years went by."

"So did I," Wren admitted, "but I didn't have much to go on, only what my foster parents told me about her."

"Would you like to see some pictures?" Zettie asked.

Wren nodded eagerly so Zettie directed Kyle to take a box down from the top of the chifferobe in the bedroom. "We'll study on some of the old photos after supper. There'll be time afore the meetin'," she added while lifting a lid from a pot on the back of the stove and testing the contents with a fork.

"Chicken's 'bout done. Winnie, would you set the table on the back porch? Kyle, how about you carryin' out the chairs? The storm's past and the evenin' air is fresh."

Wren glanced out, surprised to see sunshine shimmering on the wet leaves. The only other evidence of the storm was the many rivulets cascading into the branch that nearly encircled the back yard. Contentedly, she carried out plates and glasses and flatware while Zettie dished good smelling things into the bowls Kyle held out for her. Wren filled a pitcher from the hand pump by the kitchen sink, marveling at how cold the water was.

"It stays cold in the spring house," Zettie explained. "Your great-great papaw found this spring and it has never failed. We speculate it's part of an underground network connected with The Spring."

Wren suddenly noticed Zettie studying her shrewdly, as if taking her measure against ... what? Involuntarily, she lowered her gaze and noticed the pitcher was slipping in her hands.

But Zettie said nothing more, merely draping her apron on a nail before joining Wren and Kyle at the table outside. A pewter cup stood in the center of the table beside a plate of fluffy biscuits. "Winnie Lovada, would you bless our food this evening?" she asked.

Wren started but Kyle smiled with delight. "Me?" she asked uncertainly.

"You have that right in this house," Zettie said firmly, her air of authority surprising Wren.

Hesitantly, Wren held her hands over the table, feeling

herself directed by some larger reality. Her inner senses, already wakened by her earlier experiences in the cove, were flooded with a strange sense of power. Slowly, in response to this inner prompting, she began to pray: "God and Creator of all, bless us as we gather here to share this food that has been made holy through my, my Mamaw's loving hands. By sharing it, may we be strengthened to give and forgive...", Wren choked and struggled, as misty images of pleading figures flitted through her mind. Among them was her mother, Della. Abruptly Wren shook her head, fearful of being plunged into the eerie underworld that seemed so near again.

Kyle watched anxiously as Wren's face paled. A nimbus of light surrounded the food over which Wren's palms hovered. Ghostly hands reached for it in supplication. Suddenly, Wren sat down. Kyle and Zettie took their places in silence without commenting on Wren's unfinished prayer or her sudden pallor.

After they were seated, Zettie laid her hand lightly on her granddaughter's shoulder. "Do what you can, child," she murmured, adding firmly, "but also what you must. I feel Della movin' closer to us and I welcome her home."

Then she frowned, "I also sense something more here... something that I don't understand. A link has been established to a desperate cry from somewhere in the past." Zettie groped for further perception. "Someone, blood-kin I believe, has been overcome by something hateful. Who or when I can't make out."

Wren looked questioningly at Kyle. At his assent, she told Zettie about her recent "visions" of the frightened young woman and her conviction that the unborn infant was somehow related to her. Zettie's expression darkened.

"Do you know who the woman is?" she asked urgently.

"No," Wren confessed. Against her inclination, she tried to visualize again the scene from the previous night. "At one time she seemed to be struggling with someone tall, tall and very strong," she murmured, "That person, if it was one, seemed dark. I-I don't remember seeing a face but I definitely recall the strange timbre of the voice."

"Would you recognize that voice again?" Zettie asked.

"Yes!" Wren replied, surprised at her own certainty.

"We may need to bring this up tonight," Zettie pondered while Wren and Kyle exchanged looks of alarm.

"You mean, at the meeting?" Kyle questioned. "What is this meeting about?"

"The Cove, Lovada Cove and our life here, is being threatened," Zettie replied. "Oh, this kind of thing has happened before but most everyone senses that this time something, someone from within the group, is involved, possibly unwittingly. That's why we've summoned all the Guardians, including my two boys - your uncles, Winnie."

"Summoned?" Kyle puzzled. "How can you do that? There's no phone line or mail service back here. Are you telling me you all enjoy some kind of telepathy?"

Zettie laughed merrily. "Nothing so strange as that, Kyle. E- mail is our normal means of staying in touch."

"E-mail?" Wren sputtered through a mouthful of chicken dumplings. Kyle carefully lowered his fork, eyes wide in amazement as he pondered the incongruity as well as impossibility of it.

"Jonah picks up most of the messages," Zettie went on calmly. "His computer is pretty sophisticated, I hear. Have you been to his place yet?"

Kyle mutely shook his head.

"You cain't hardly miss it," Zettie went on, "his roof and yard are cluttered with solar panels that feed energy into his generator. Of course, here in the Smokies you can't count on enough sunlight to keep the batteries charged up so he and the Garenflo brothers rigged up some business with the water wheel at the old gristmill. I imagine that's churning right strong after this rainstorm, " Zettie reflected. "I don't really understand it all myself but Clyde used to spend a lot of time over with Jonah when they was workin' to get the steady flow of electricity that computers need. He picks up signals from the radio towers on the peaks nearby. Guess it's something like cell phones do?"

Kyle took a swallow of water. "You really do have email capability, then? Somehow," he glanced about Zettie's kitchen with its primitive facilities, "it doesn't seem to fit. I'd begun to think you folks were like the Old Amish, not trusting new technology."

"Oh, we have nothing against progress that brings folks closer together," Zettie commented calmly. "It's been real helpful what with Cove Communities scattered all over as they are."

"Cove Communities? Bewley referred to them when he was telling us the story of Lovada Branch," Wren recounted.

"I'm beginning to think he didn't tell us half of all that's going on," Kyle commented wryly.

"Like as not," Zettie agreed as she rose to clear the table. "You'll learn more at the meetin' tonight."

Once her kitchen was put to rights, Zettie fetched an album from the box Kyle had taken from the chifferobe and led them out to the front porch, still bright in the westering sun. Easing herself into a rocker, she opened the book on her lap with Kyle and Wren hanging over her shoulders.

The earliest pictures were faded daguerreotypes, taken mainly at weddings and funerals. Zettie pointed to one of the earliest, a wedding photo with the husband seated, the bride in black standing with her hand on his shoulder. The couple stared out so stiffly that Wren wondered if their heads were clamped into position. Despite the formality of the pose, she detected a serenity in their eyes that probed and challenged her. There was something vaguely familiar about the woman whose blond hair was swept up into a bun.

Zettie glanced up at Wren. "Yes, that's your great-granny and namesake, Winnie Lovada."

"Your parents then?" Wren asked.

"Yes, but I don't remember my Maw very clearly. She died in childbirth when I was about two. Pa never got over it. He'd talk of her sometimes - like she'd just been a week gone. Used to tell of the spells she'd get."

"Spells?" Wren echoed.

"Twern't all that uncommon," Zettie went on, "leastways not among Lovada women. Made him nervous, of course, especially after she told him somethin' awful was 'bout to happen in the Borderlands. She was right, too."

"The massacre at the Bentley place?" Kyle interrupted.

"Yep, and it grieved her terrible," Zettie admitted, "being she was a Bentley on her Ma's side."

"Couldn't she have warned them?" Wren asked.

"Don't know about that," Zettie replied thoughtfully. "She may have tried but you know how folks can be. Won't believe a thing there's no proof for."

Zettie turned some pages and showed them a photo of her three children, the two boys on either side of their younger sister. Wren studied Della curiously. Porter's arm rested casually across her shoulders. Della stood with her arms crossed stiffly on her chest, her mouth set in a grim line unexpected for a girl her age. So this was her mother.

"No question you favor her," Kyle observed. "That picture of her at twelve could be you. Including," he added teasingly, "that stubborn look."

Wren stiffened. This was the woman she had accused most of her life. Had she been blaming part of herself?

Zettie pointed to another photo of a teen-age girl with permed hair, dressed in late fifties style. "That was Della after she went to work over in Black Mountain," Zettie said. "A number of craft shops were opening as the tourist trade

83

spread out from Lashton. Della took a job there as soon as she turned sixteen. Almost never came home after that...

Zettie paused, remembering. "Strange how quick she left... like she was running from somethin'. More likely to someone? She had just told us that a young man, a potter or sculptor or some such, was promisin' her a ring. I recollect that really riled Porter. Said she had no business marryin' an out-lander." Zettie sighed. "Della offered to bring her young man back here to The Cove the next time we went. Clyde had his doubts about that but Della insisted that she wanted to marry her man before the elders in the church here."

"Was that the custom?" Wren asked.

"Depended," Zettie said cryptically.

"Did they marry here in The Cove?" Kyle asked.

"No, not to my knowledge," Zettie admitted sadly. "We didn't see Della again for about six months. Then she came back like I told you, all broken up but wouldn't stay with us. She went on to Lashton and this letter she wrote after Winnie's birth is the last we ever heard from her."

Zettie plucked a folded paper from the album in her lap and handed it to Wren, who took it with trembling hands. It was the only thing of her mother's that she had ever touched. The cheap paper had yellowed but the faded ballpoint script was still legible. *"Dear Ma and Pa, Two days ago, I had a beautiful baby girl and she seems perfect in every way. I hardly dare believe she is all right. I named her Winnie Lovada after Mamaw. I'll bring her home to you as soon as I can but I have to do something first. If it doesn't work out... well, I don't want to think about that. Pray for me and for little Winnie. Your loving daughter, Della Lovada.*

Wren's voice quivered. "She thought I was beautiful," she murmured. "She wanted to bring me home to her folks. Oh, if only she had! What happened?"

Zettie wiped tears from her eyes. "We don't know. Like

I said, we kep' watchin' for her to come, even after we moved back here from Viney Branch. The boys tried to track her down (and you, of course) but didn't get very far. Your Uncle Locke asked at the hospital but they wouldn't give out any records, even when he said he was Della's brother. Porter, he tried too. Somehow, your name never got registered at the courthouse."

"My foster parents never bothered with that when they decided to keep me after it was clear my mother had abandoned me. So they changed my name to Wren Linda," Wren explained. "But why would my Ma just leave like that? I always figured she hated me for some reason."

Kyle walked over to the edge of the porch and stared out into the twilight. "You don't have any idea what it was Della had to do, do you?" he asked casually of Zettie. When the older woman didn't answer, he turned to pursue the question but just then a bell rang out from the church steeple.

"The Meetin'!" Zettie gasped and struggled up from the rocking chair.

CHAPTER EIGHT

In the twilight, Kyle made out people converging on the white chapel from all directions. He easily recognized Oma's stout figure accompanied by the lanky Anson Jack. Jonah's burly form strode purposefully across the far field. Kyle figured the gray blur flowing past the laurel was probably Mencie and the two older men could be the Garenflo brothers. Bewley and Haidia emerged from the woods between the chapel and Zettie's place. The rest of the men and women were unknown but somehow, not unfamiliar. There was something about the people of this cove that was so comfortable Kyle felt he had grown up among them.

Eight or ten people were hurrying across the meadow from the direction of the notch. A few waved to Zettie as she, with Wren and Kyle in tow, set out briskly for the meeting. There was little talk - as if those approaching the chapel were absorbed in some sort of inner preparation for this gathering. Everyone was middle-aged or older, Kyle noted, once he entered the building where oil lamps glowed softly along the walls.

Wren was pleased to see that both men and women used both doorways and that no dour-faced beadle hovered in the shadows. She and Kyle slipped into one of the back pews while Zettie hurried forward to greet two men, one in denim jeans; the other taller one, in a suit jacket. Seeing them in profile, Wren noted that the farmer in particular resembled herself, his short stature a match for her own. Both men had reddish hair.

"My uncles!" she thought with a thrill of recognition, men- tally rehearsing what Zettie had told her about her boys-Locke, the bachelor farmer; Porter, the school principal and family man. They were absorbed in earnest conversation with their mother but at one point, Porter looked back over the crowded nave, searching until his eyes fell on Wren. He smiled and raised his hand in a brief wave before Zettie, tugging on his arm, whispered something about "later." Locke merely squinted at Wren with a grim expression.

Gradually, the steady tapping of footfalls diminished. The chapel was full, a few latecomers slipping in beside Kyle and Wren. A hush fell over the gathering like a blanket, a waiting that was both relaxed and expectant. This silence was not merely an absence of speech, Wren realized. Everyone there was actively listening. Wren felt herself being absorbed by the same power. Beside her Kyle's breathing deepened and slowed as he, too, was caught up in the stillness.

Wren closed her eyes, losing track of time and place, until a stir as of a light breeze passed over the people. Looking up, she saw a thin woman with short gray hair walking toward the pulpit. She wore a well-washed housedress and sneakers. Others noticed her and raised their heads as she picked up a large Bible from a table and leafed through it thoughtfully before turning to place it on the podium.

"I counsel we listen again to these words," she began,

her full, rich voice penetrating every corner of the chapel.

"What I am doing is sending you out like sheep among wolves. You must be clever as snakes and innocent as doves. Be on your guard with respect to others...."

The woman threw a penetrating gaze out over the gathering and Wren was surprised by the imperative in her eyes. Moving her finger down the page, the woman continued: *"Do not worry about what you will say or how you will say it. When the hour comes, you will be given what you are to say. You yourselves will not be the speakers; the Spirit of your Father will be speaking in you. Brother will hand over brother ... the father, his child...."*

The reader's voice slowed and when she glanced up again, Kyle noted that her eyes seemed to settle on Wren, arousing an uncomfortable premonition in Kyle. After a pause, she continued in a more confident tone.

"Do not let them intimidate you."

No one in the chapel stirred as the woman slowly turned the page and smoothed it down with her hand. Softly now, she asked, *"Are not two sparrows sold for next to nothing? Yet not a single sparrow falls to the ground without your Father's consent. As for you, every hair of your head has been counted; so do not be afraid of anything."*

Solemnly the reader lifted the book high and everyone present stood and bowed. Wren and Kyle heard a rush of whispered responses from those around them as the woman left the pulpit. "That there is Tishie, one of our Faith-Keepers," the woman next to Wren murmured, adding with gossipy helpfulness, 'When she's moved to read, we all know somethin' mighty is in the wind."

Kyle barely heard the woman's explanation for the words of Matthew's Gospel were exploding within him like skyrockets. The words were familiar enough but never before had he felt them so directed at him. His mind reeled; his heart hammered. Beside him, Wren uttered a small moan as if she sensed a personal threat in these words.

"If I really believed those words," Kyle reflected to himself, "I wouldn't be hiding who and what I am." A vision of his life lived openly, freed from guilt and anger, no longer twisted by conflict, astounded him. If he really believed those words, accepted them, he could stand tall and speak the truths he knew without fear. Nothing would prevent him living out his deepest call, not even his own guilt.

How liberating, this image of a life without fear or conflict, of a life of truth and harmony! Was it this that made the people in The Cove so different? So genuinely caring? *"Perfect love casts out fear."* What would such love look like, feel like, sound like? Kyle doubted he had ever encountered it. Perhaps he would not even have recognized it if he had. But here... now....

A man in jeans strode forward from the back of the church, the heels of his boots ringing on the wood floor. His broad, dark features and blue-black hair pulled back in a ponytail proclaimed him as Cherokee. "One of the Guardians," the helpful lady at Wren's side volunteered.

The man turned when he reached the chancel step. "Folks, not all of you know why you were summoned here tonight. I know some of the reasons but clearly there are more as Tishie has warned us through these words from The Book."

He paused briefly and glanced around. "We all know Lovada Cove is officially federal park land and under the jurisdiction of the Forest Service. Recently the Service has negotiated with Boxer Paper Mill to log Unaka Mountain." A collective gasp rose from the gathering. "And... they have also granted mineral rights to some mining ventures."

Stunned, people stirred and murmured, incensed by such a violation of protected, and to them, sacred land. Kyle's eyes flashed with indignation and his grip on Wren's hand tightened until she winced.

"No need to fret over our folks here in The Cove," the man went on. "You have our assurance as Guardians, the community will be provided for as it has been in the past. What we need to consider is how to protect the mountain itself. The innocence of doves is not enough at this moment; we are asked to exercise the cleverness of snakes."

Wren stirred uncomfortably when Kyle squeezed harder, nodding in agreement.

A man in the center of the church stood to address the speaker. "Jerry, this here's a puzzle. We all want to defend Unaka Mountain, but how? Violence will gain us nothin' but more violence. Has the Mountain told you what is expected of us?"

Jerry nodded slowly and his eyes glazed over, becoming dark and distant. Rocking slowly back and forth he intoned:

"Listen! Listen to what Father Unaka is saying to us.
'Sing! Sing of me, strongly and sweetly;
sing of my strength and sing of my fragility.
An old, old mountain am I;
Many the changes I have seen and endured.
Many my scars
but time heals them all.
I can survive what loggers and miners might do.
But can you?"

Jerry's eyes glowed as the rhythmic chant flowed from his mouth.

"Your time, oh humans, is brief,
like the doe that flees across the grass.
You need me much more than I need you.
Children, for your own sake
And for the sake of your sons and daughters,
do all you can now.

90

Sing of me!
Sing of me gently and joyously, sing without fear.
sing with power and with strength.
Sing simply so many will join your song.
Spin out your song endlessly
until those against me tire.
Rest only when the birds and breezes prolong your song
forever free and wild."

Many nods greeted Jerry's words but no one spoke. Through the open windows drifted the call of the whip-poor-will and a concert of red wolves. Kyle recognized the musical yipping and rejoiced to know a remnant pack did indeed remain, roaming the perimeter of The Cove.

Kyle's instinctive reaction to begin planning petition drives; organize mailings; hammer at the bureaucracy suffered a shock. Sing? Was that all? What could that accomplish? He clenched and unclenched his fist as an inherited wisdom warred with all the smarts of the culture in which he had grown up. Was life a vicious battle with victory going only to the strongest or more wily? Or was there another Way?

As Kyle felt the axis of his inner world tilting, the music of the mountain outside the chapel windows grew louder. Not only were the birds and the insects singing but the trees and grasses and rocks added their own harmonics. Kyle sucked in his breath. The very earth beneath his feet thrummed with life. Whoever interpreted and sang this for others would have done enough. The Mountain needed no other defense. It was what it was forever.

Kyle's reflections were interrupted when a man's voice cut harshly through the chapel. "I don't agree that song is sufficient. We are dealing with the rape of this ancient and sacred mountain

...mebbe loss of The Cove itself. Not just us here but

everything we foster in the larger world is at risk. I believe in the power of music but not all of us are musicians. We need to show love, active love for these misguided people. Do them good! What do they need that we can offer them?"

Kyle's stomach contracted and beside him, Wren's sharp inhalation was audible. Just what were they being challenged to do? Though he and Wren had spent barely twenty-four hours in The Cove, he found himself identifying with these people as his own. What affected the Lovada Cove community was now his personal concern as well. Kyle leaned forward to study Ollie, the elderly man who had challenged Jerry.

Ollie hitched one of his red braces higher on his shoulder and continued. "I sense we're dealin' with somethin' larger than jest greed and grabbin' here, somethin' dark, somethin' mean-minded. More than song is needed now. A time of trial and testin' is to hand here, would you know. How say you?"

Slowly Zettie rose and joined Jerry on the chancel step. Standing beside the broad Cherokee, she looked even tinier, but her voice was firm and clear. "Ollie, you're on to somethin' but it's a truth hard to figure. What's happenin' now couldn't have gone this far, come this close, without our knowing of it 'less'n ...," Zettie bit her lip and smoothed down the front of her dress. "less'n it comes from roots that been a-growin' fer years. I don't fully understand the trouble myself. What I suspicion is ... is," Zettie's voice broke and Jerry put his hand under her elbow to steady her. She took a deep breath and plunged on, "that it has lodged in my family and will require someone of our blood to heal it."

Wren noticed her Uncle Locke blanche under his tan and his neck muscles bulge. Porter sat motionless, eyes focused on his mother who continued hoarsely, "Lovada Cove's danger is mortal; we heal this now or we die, one." Shock swept through the chapel but no one spoke. "Who has love enough to kiss a betrayer?"

Tishie, the woman who had read earlier, crossed swiftly over to Zettie and embraced her, whispering urgently. The older woman, head down, nodded. Tishie turned, her eyes sweeping over the congregation until she found Wren and Kyle. With a lift of her chin, she summoned them.

Wren felt ghostly hands suddenly pressing her down into the pew, dragging her through the flooring and into the dark world she had twice fled in terror. From a great distance, she heard Zettie's voice. "Let us all join in prayer for Winnie Lovada and Kyle Makepeace, sent to us in our hour of need."

As murmured prayers flowed around her, Wren felt herself released from the grasping hands and restored to the peaceful glow of the chapel. She and Kyle heard the people gathering in protective circles around them. Arms were raised in invocation, creating a shield against a power that suddenly seemed to hurl itself like a furious storm against the walls of the chapel. The praying group huddled together like ancient cave dwellers, sustaining one another by shared body heat. The old stone of the mountain joined with the strength of the ageless oak and the relentless force of water gushing from high springs. Even so, Kyle felt the bulwark shudder as if the blasts being hurled repeatedly against it sought fissures that could weaken it. Would it hold? Could it hold? He gripped Wren's hand and pulled her close.

Mencie's voice echoed as the chapel darkened, "Pray, pray with all your strength for they are working against us this night."

"What shall we pray against?" Wren cried out in anguish, as she felt her body and spirit being overtaken by forces she could neither resist nor trust.

"Pray against nothing!" Mencie urged. "Pray that what you hear the darkness demand, you may have the courage to expose to the light."

At her words, the defenses surrounding Wren and Kyle ceased wavering and became clearly, strongly focused. Encompassed now as by an impregnable tower, Wren knew she was being asked to find again the despairing, frightened woman of her earlier "dreams." It should have been a simple thing, haunted as she was by the experience but now a door had slammed shut. She was being deliberately prevented from reaching her again.

"Kyle! I can't find her. Something is keeping me out." Wren cried in panic. "What can I do?"

Kyle tightened his grip on Wren's hand. As he looked into her eyes, flooded with fear and desperation, long-suppressed memories surged up in him. He had seen that same fear in... no! he dared not let himself remember for the guilt and shame were too great. He had not done then what he should have. And someone had died. No second chance was possible for him, was it?

Just as he was about to release Wren's fingers and turn from her, the power of the gathered prayer seeped into his racked soul. He could not fail someone he loved again. He would not!

Hesitantly, Kyle reached for the fringed pouch hanging around his neck. He didn't trust himself to deal with the herb it contained and thought to hand it over to Jerry who was undoubtedly more skilled and more worthy. As he lifted the cord over his head, he found Jonah at his side. But when he offered the pouch to Jerry who now stood beside Jonah, the elder shook his head and folded Kyle's own hand around it. Mencie set a clay pot filled with red coals at Kyle's feet and handed him a raven feather.

Gentle hands helped Wren to sit on the floor while Kyle rocked back on his heels, conflict written on his face. No! He could not accept this function. He had renounced it long ago. But when Wren moaned in despair, he sprinkled a few flakes of the dried herb on the coals and carefully wafted the pungent smoke into her face. After a few breaths, her eyes glazed and her body went limp. Zettie knelt behind Wren's back, supporting her firmly.

Wren felt herself slipping deeper into a chill darkness that smelled of mold and death. She was in a tomb and panic overtook her. But the acrid smoke from the clay pot burned her nostrils and she opened her eyes to find herself rocking to and fro in a dark, moist prison. An impassioned voice was murmuring words she could not understand, though she felt they were terribly important. In spirit she stretched out her hand toward that voice. In a remote region of her awareness, fingers connected with hers.

In the chapel, Kyle watched Wren's body jerk upright, her eyes unfocused. Zettie hovered protectively behind her while around them the group chanted softly, the melody a sustaining and guiding influence, as Kyle carefully dribbled a few more flakes of the herb into the smoldering pot.

"She found it for me," Wren began tonelessly. "She was on her way back with it when she was overcome ... she was alone but not for long. Others ... others reached her but it was too late. She was afraid and wanted to protect me, help me... but how could she... after what had happened to her?"

"Who wished to protect you?" Zettie prompted softly.

"Della Lovada," Wren continued in a flat voice. "When she knew she was pregnant, she tried to come back to The Cove. She got as far as the Bentley place but could not get through the Barrier carrying what she had. So she went back to Lashton, deciding to wait until after I was born ...."

When Wren's toneless recital ceased, the murmuring chant of the group continued, winding over, around, and under the words that hung on the still air. Zettie risked another question. "And afterward, did she come back again?"

"Yes... it's all a mist... a mist," Wren cried out wildly.

Kyle leaned forward, uncertain whether to intrude or not but knowing how urgently they needed the information that Wren was fighting to disclose. "Do you know where she is now? Can you find her?"

"Yes-s-s," Wren responded. Her body jerked as if something had tried to prevent her answering Kyle. The pulse of the chant quickened as if all were aware of an increased threat and Wren's body quieted.

"Did she tell anyone what she knew?" Zettie asked softly. Wren struggled but exhaustion overtook her and her eyes fluttered shut. Kyle's heart almost stopped as he feared she, too, had been found and overcome in the mists. Someone knelt beside him, steadying him.

Quickly Jerry sealed Kyle's pouch shut and took the raven feather from his stiff fingers. Then he laid dried sweet grass and sage on the still burning coals and as they began to smolder, waved the smoke into Wren's face. Zettie whispered, "Do not let anyone intimidate you, child. Do not fear those who can deprive your body of life but cannot touch your soul." She stroked Wren's head tenderly. "Every hair on your head has been counted. Do not be afraid of anything, dear one."

Wren's breathing deepened, color returned to her face and when she opened her eyes, Kyle could see the remnants of her panic receding. "Do you remember anything?" he inquired, taking her hand gently into his own.

"Yes, I remember," she said sadly. "Now I have to find her for I must finish what she could not."

Around them the chanting changed as if a storm had passed and sunlight were breaking through clouds. Though still solemn and urgent, syllables of "alleluia" were interspersed with phrases from Mencie's song: "Are you here at His rising from the dead?"

Zettie walked Kyle and Wren to the front of the chapel,

flanked by Locke and Porter. The rest of the gathering settled again in their seats as Jonah took Jerry's place on the chancel step.

"The Lord is here among us," he began, his eyes saluting all the faces turned toward him. "This evening He is calling another of His anointed to a change of heart."

Jonah held out his hand to Kyle, summoning him to his side. Kyle shook his head so sharply his thick silvery hair fell across his brow. "No! Not now, not ever!" He leapt aside, balancing on the balls of his feet, about to pivot and cut out of the chapel. But before he could move, several men and women raised their arms in blessing.

Wordlessly, they laid their hands on Kyle's head, forcing him down to his knees. He quivered as each person's touch stirred to life portions of his spirit he had sworn would never live again. One last touch jolted him with a power so strong and familiar, Kyle cried out in shock. It was Wren, smoothing his hair gently but firmly into place. Kyle wanted to jump up and shake her, try to stop her. But the Power flowing back and forth between them paralyzed him.

The burdens Kyle had once rejected were being returned to him. He was confused, humbled, angry, not ready for this. Only someone with integrity, with undivided loyalties, should so serve. "No, Lord, not me! Not again." he groaned.

Jonah touched him lightly. "Do you refuse?"

Kyle shook his head miserably. "No ... yes. Would that I could! Why won't He let me go?"

Tishie's rich voice suddenly filled the chapel:

"It shall come to pass in the last days, says God, that I will pour out a portion of my spirit on all humanity. Your sons and daughters shall prophesy, your young men shall see visions and your old men shall dream dreams. Yes, even on my servants and handmaids I will pour out a portion of my spirit in those days, and they shall prophesy."

Wren watched as Kyle raised his head, the glow from the lamps glistening like oil on his silvery hair. Around her, The Cove community waited expectantly. Kyle looked deeply into Wren's eyes and she recoiled from the torment mirrored there. He looked like a man just plunged into boiling oil. His nails dug into her shoulder like talons and she knew that at this moment he hated her and all her kin.

Compassionately, Jonah slid his hand over Kyle's and led him quietly out of the church. No one moved or spoke but a wave of tenderness so powerful that even Kyle felt it, swept through the chapel. The people were praying again.

Wren remained close to Zettie, confused, grateful, willing to trust the Power that surrounded her and Kyle. Gradually the people resettled themselves in the pews. Oma stepped into the pulpit. Solemnly she stretched her arms out over the assembly:

"By waiting and by calm we shall be saved, in quiet and in trust our strength lies. May the Lord bless us and keep us. May he show his face to us and be merciful to us. May we always be eager to serve the Lord in one another for the Lord is here among us and we are always with him. Amen."

People began to file out, their faces peaceful and their voices gentle as they encouraged Wren who remained sheltered in Zettie's embrace. As the chapel emptied, Porter and Locke joined the two women and Wren met her uncles for the first time.

CHAPTER NINE

Locke pulled a large flashlight from his pocket and shone it on the road as they left the chapel and wended their way back toward Zettie's little cabin. Wren was relieved when Jonah, with Kyle in tow, joined them. As her eyes adjusted to the dim light, she tried to read Kyle's face but could discern little more than his rigid jaw line. Both of them had been touched by live currents of spiritual energies which had left them raw and reeling. It was soothing to walk along the cove road towards Zettie's homey cabin.

The night was starry and fresh after the afternoon storm, alive with fireflies rising like sparks from the grassy pastures along the road. No one spoke as they walked through the gentle May night, each one pondering the events of the meeting. Though Kyle moved to Wren's side, he made no attempt to touch her. He seemed as aware as she, that nothing, including their marriage, would ever be the same again.

Jonah excused himself when they reached Zettie's porch and strode off across the meadow toward his own place. Zettie soon settled her family around her table with mugs of fragrant mint tea and fresh cookies. Porter frankly studied Wren, taking in her slender figure and bouncy auburn curls. "Maw was right," he announced, "you sure do put us in mind of Della. Seem to have a lot of her feisty spirit, too."

Wren tried to relax against her chair, absorbing the sensation of sharing a table with three blood relatives. Staring into her steaming mug, she murmured, "Learning about all of you now after so long ... I don't know what to do with it yet. And," she paused, uncertain about this admission, "I don't know what to think of Della ... my mother, your... your sister, anymore. I'm so used to being angry at her that now I feel empty, like this great anger is melting away and there's nothing to fill the vacuum... yet. It shakes me up to think that she died trying to spare me from something. I know I should be grateful, love her even... but there's still too much I don't understand."

"She loved you," Zettie observed, "but despite that, she hurt you in ways that have left scars you'll always have to live with. Not because she wanted to ... I suspicion she wanted to spare you from even worse pain." Zettie studied her gnarled hands helplessly before adding softly, "There's things I feel I should have known...."

Locke, who had been watching Wren through slitted eyes, grunted suddenly and turned away from the table. Unlike Porter who had welcomed her so warmly, Locke emanated a coolness that hurt and puzzled Wren. Of the two brothers, he most resembled her, being short and wiry with reddish hair on his balding head.

Now he broke in harshly, as if eager to change the drift of the conversation. "I've been studying on what all happened there in church and reckon that the sad woman you've connected with is likely Della."

Everyone in the room reacted as if Locke had laid a dead possum on the table. Porter clenched his fist and glared at his brother. Kyle moved closer to Wren who had shrunk back in her chair and Zettie simply moaned softly. Heedlessly, Locke plunged on. "You'll want to be looking for her. That could be dangerous and I don't recommend it. Might be better if you'ns jest left it to me. I know these parts pretty good and have the time now that the 'bacca is set."

Kyle felt a surge of irritation, suspecting that Locke was deliberately hiding something. "Thanks for nothing, Locke," he responded roughly, "but this is something we should handle."

Wren frowned at Locke and reiterated Kyle's words, "I don't know exactly what we will meet up with but this is something we have to do ourselves."

Abruptly, Locke kicked back from the table, emptied his cup in the sink and stalked out the door. Kyle noted the glitter in Porter's eyes and wondered at his wary silence during this exchange.

Zettie's anxious eyes flickered over them and she sighed, as if all too familiar with this kind of bickering. "You'ns can stay here for the night, if you care to. We can open up the couch in the living room for Winnie and Kyle while the boys can stay in their old room."

Porter cleared his throat. 'I'd like to stay, Maw, but school's back in session after the break for spring planting. I need to get back home tonight. Besides, Jonah asked me to check out what the Forest Service is up to. Seems like they've got a new strategy, sending scouts into the woods to mark where the logging road will go through so they can get the dozer's rolling in before anyone knows what's going on."

Kyle was suddenly alert. "What's this about scouts? Who are they using?"

"Mostly Cherokee who always hunted back in here," Porter responded, eyeing Kyle speculatively.

"That might explain it," Kyle said thoughtfully. "Wren and I heard some cardinal calls this afternoon on our way over from Bewley and Haidia's. They reminded me of what my Dad and I used to do when we got separated while out hunting. I knew there was something wrong about those

101

whistles. Maybe it was the scouts working their way through?"

Locke, who had silently returned to the kitchen, scowled, "You said that was between here and Bewley's place? If those were signals you were hearing, the scouts are nearer than we figured."

"How close can they get to The Cove and not find you folks?" Kyle asked anxiously.

Zettie reached over and patted his hand. "Don't you fret about us, son. We have our ways."

Wren shivered and set her mug down so quickly some of the tea splashed out. Despite the warmth of Zettie's kitchen, a black miasma seemed to cloud the air, accompanied by the now familiar odor of mold and decay. Kyle regarded Wren with concern.

"I have a bad feeling about this," she said. "I don't know what your "ways" are, Mamaw, but tell me this. Could you all be found if someone from among you wanted that to happen?"

"You mean, one of us betrayed our own kin?" Porter asked incredulously.

Zettie looked solemn. "It's the only way, son."

"That's it, Kyle," Wren moaned, "That's what the Powers wanted Della to do. And that's what I am destined to do." She stuffed her fist against her mouth, eyes wide with regret and pain.

"Now wait a minute," Porter began, 'there's something here we're forgetting. Della found something, you said, something you implied could prevent this betrayal."

"Ye--es, but we'll never find Della in time," Wren added hopelessly.

"Don't be so sure," Porter said slowly, "Did she lose whatever it is she found?"

"No, she didn't," Wren responded, surprised by her own certainty.

Kyle rolled his mug between his hands. "Maybe we are meant to find Della ... and maybe, just maybe, it could make a difference."

"And maybe I won't have to betray The Cove and my ... my folks?" Wren asked with a hint of hope in her voice.

"We don't know how or when Della will be found," Zettie mused, "but Winnie's right about this. She's the one who must do it. T'won't be easy. But it can be done." She nodded, "Yes, it can be done ...."

Locke made an impatient gesture. "Leave it! There's other ways to save The Cove."

Kyle covertly studied Locke, his suspicions rising about why this older brother was so anxious to prevent their searching for Della on their own. What did the man guess or perhaps, know... that they did not?

Porter glared at his brother, "Stay out of this, Locke. I know better than you what all is going on here."

Locke narrowed his eyes and studied his brother briefly in such stone-faced rage that Kyle sensed he was about to strike him and only Zettie's wordless gesture of peace prevented him.

In the uneasy silence that followed, Porter cleared his throat nervously and began, "I'm going back to Laurel Spring tonight. Tomorrow I'll talk with some of the fellas I know who work for the Forest Service. They owe me so I figure they'll tell me fairly straight what's going on. In the morning Wren and Kyle can go looking for Della. Maw will tell the rest of The Cove what they are doing so the community can help."

Kyle protested, "A crowd of folks beating the bushes out there might do more harm than good."

Porter and Zettie shook their heads. "That's not the kind of help we're talking about." Despite Kyle's raised eyebrows, Porter did not elaborate but continued ticking off items on his fingers.

"At the same time, some of the Guardians who were here tonight will be contacting our best balladeers and pickers and cloggers to get out and start making music about the mountain. It won't be long before the whole state knows that Unaka Mountain needs saving. With that kind of knowing, we can do much," Porter concluded.

Kyle gazed appraisingly at Porter, irritated again by the man's easy assumption of authority. Plans were taking shape so smoothly ... too smoothly, Kyle thought, and he frowned just as Wren looked his way. Disturbed by Kyle's signal of mistrust of her newly found uncle, Wren turned to Porter, reaching out to touch his arm gratefully. He stroked her slender fingers briefly before rising from the table.

Zettie disappeared into the bedroom, returning with a bundle of fresh sheets and towels that she gave to Wren and Kyle. While the two of them wrestled the fold-up couch into a bed, she cleared the kitchen. Porter set off into the night in the direction of the notch.

After several nights in sleeping bags, the prospect of a bed with sheets held a delicious appeal for Kyle and Wren. They settled in quickly and gratefully but as Kyle began to turn down the wick on the oil lamp, Wren touched his arm.

"I need to ask you about something."

Kyle sat up seeking to cradle Wren against his chest but she pulled away stiffly "What's on your mind, honey?" he murmured.

"Too much," she retorted, scrubbing her hands impatiently through her hair. But for a few minutes she said nothing more, waiting in silence until they heard Locke come in and retire into a back bedroom. Already, Zettie was beginning to snore and whiffle from her room off the kitchen.

"Kyle, so many things are churning around in me that I can't sort out anything. But one thing really bothers me. I saw the way you looked at my uncles tonight. They were trying to help us and you kept putting them off. You don't trust my people, do you." It was a statement, not a question.

Kyle hesitated, "You must admit, Wren, that this whole place and everyone in it are mighty strange. We just met Locke and Porter; we hardly know Zettie yet. At every turn, things get more and more bizarre. What do you expect?"

Wren tossed her head in frustration. 'Kyle! How can I know? Already things aren't the same between us. I'm finding out things about you that you never told me. I hate that kind of deceit."

"Deceit?" Kyle retorted."Seems to me that until now you didn't much care about my past. You certainly never asked to know more."

"Did I have to? I trusted you to tell me all I should know about you. Now I suspect you only told me as much as you wanted me to know. Have you more dark secrets, Kyle Makepeace? Seems like you don't trust me any more than the rest of my family!"

Kyle dropped his head and studied his hands. "I do trust you, Wren, but ... well, there's things I just don't talk about with anyone ... too complicated and ... too painful."

Relentlessly, Wren pushed on. "Too hard to share even with your wife? Who else did I have but you? And now that I've finally found some people I can call my own, I do believe you're jealous."

Kyle studied the jut of Wren's jaw and sighed. Past experience had taught him that Wren would hear little or nothing of what he had to say when her quick temper was aroused. In this, she seemed to resemble her Uncle Locke all too closely.

"Wren, can this wait?" he pleaded. "We've both been through some pretty rough stuff in the past twenty-four hours. I'm not ready to deal with these questions. Neither are you, if you are honest."

Wren snorted. "Honesty? How can you talk about that to me? Can't you see what it's been like for me, never having any true family for so long and now...." Abruptly Wren turned away and flopped down on her side, her back to Kyle.

Kyle eyed the stiffness in her shoulders warily. How could he reach her? Hesitantly, he caressed the reddish gleams in her hair. Wren's fierce defense of her people was understand-able but he hoped her trust was not so blind... Wren's hand stole up and covered his briefly in a small gesture of reconciliation. He risked kissing it before blowing out the light and settling down silently at her side.

CHAPTER TEN

Kyle felt he had barely drifted off to sleep when he was startled awake. A shadow on the windowsill was clawing at the screen. Luminous eyes gleamed in the semi-dark of the May night. Only when he glimpsed the long, fluffy tail did Kyle recognize The Dean.

"What the hell ...?" Kyle muttered, as he leapt out of bed, determined to either pitch the cat back into the night or strangle it outright.

"What's up?" Wren murmured sleepily.

"Just that damn cat scratching at the screen."

"The Dean?" Wren turned over quickly. "Kyle, that's it! That's the Summons. If we don't go now, it could be too late."

The certainty in Wren's voice troubled Kyle but he well knew she would brook no argument. Muttering about the stubbornness of an unnamed person, Kyle groped around in the dark for boots and clothes. The couple were just slipping out the front door when Zettie emerged from the kitchen.

Waving aside explanations about this midnight excursion, she reached up and traced a cross on each of their foreheads. "Go with God." she prayed softly and then hugged them both. "I'll tell Locke in the morning," she added.

"Don't bother," Kyle growled under his breath.

The Dean was waiting for them on the front porch and set out towards the woods tail high, moonlight glinting off his eyes when he glanced back at them. Wren and Kyle stumbled behind. "Talk about trust! This is insane," Kyle grumbled. "Now we're following this damn tomcat who's probably just on the prowl for his lady love."

Nearing the thick undergrowth, they spied a soft glow among the trees. Mencie awaited them with a lantern. "Follow me, if you please," she announced.

Wren stifled a nervous giggle at this conjunction of old-world formality with a midnight thrash through underbrush. Swiftly Mencie guided them to a path so narrow Kyle figured it was a game trail - small game, he realized wryly as branches whipped across his face. Wren walked with one arm raised shielding her eyes as briars snagged her hair and clothes. They crossed a small branch bubbling along its stony bed and then began to climb out of The Cove. As far as Kyle could ascertain, they were opposite the notch and moving in the direction of the old railroad line.

To his trained ear, the woods seemed unnaturally still. No scurrying of night creatures through dry leaves; no chirping of nocturnal birds watching for prey broke the silence. Even the leaves hung motionless as if the forest itself were in suspense. A chill crept up his back and neck.

Wren, walking ahead of him, appeared oblivious to the eerie quiet. Mists began to swirl among the tree trunks, diffusing the small light from Mencie's lantern into a fey gleam bobbing ahead of them. As the fog thickened, Kyle reached out to rest his hand on Wren's shoulder. The hand she laid over his was cold and clammy.

The cry of a screech owl nearly plucked Kyle out of his skin. He kicked up against Wren's heels when she stopped abruptly, smothering a shriek. Mencie, too, had halted.

"We are getting closer," she whispered, and doused the lantern. The mist pressed down on them, opaque and smothering. Kyle's hypersensitive hearing caught a soft flutter as the owl flew low over their heads.

Feeling their way forward step by step, Mencie led Wren and Kyle to the edge of a clearing. Stark in the moonlight, an abandoned cabin sagged, smothered by kudzu vines.

"Tis the Waitsel homestead," Mencie whispered.

Wren's fingers tightened on Kyle's hand and he knew she was bracing herself for whatever they would meet in this cheerless clearing. Stepping out from the rim of trees, they felt the mists form a wall behind them. Within the glade, where not a wisp of fog lingered, every sight and sound was sharply defined. The crunching of their boots on scattered debris was disturbingly loud as they circled the ruined cabin to what had been the front door. Reflexively, Wren withdrew the silver disk from her shirt, holding it before her as a shield.

"This is where she was lost," Wren said in the toneless voice Kyle recognized from her earlier tranced state. Wren moved forward as if blind, her hand stretching toward the splintered doorframe. Stones that had once formed steps to the sill were tumbled to one side. Wren paused uncertainly. She sniffed, lifting her nose in the air and Kyle noted that her eyes were glazed. Only a thread of awareness connected him to her and he focused on it. There was no response from Wren.

Wren, leaning forward, caught a whiff of mold and decay emanating from the black hole of the doorway. She wavered, seized by an overwhelming impulse to flee to safety behind a nearby pile of stones. Wrestling with the conviction that many of her questions about Della might be answered within the tomblike cabin, Wren nevertheless succumbed to her panic and reeled back from the doorway toward the rock cairn.

109

As she did so, an eerie sense of *Deja vu* seized Wren. Somehow she knew she was entering into Della's panicked moments over thirty years ago. Frantically, Wren ducked behind the four-foot heap of stones as the night dissolved into a murky memory of a berserk figure leaping upon her.

"I've been waiting for you, Winnie Lovada, waiting too long," a voice harsh with pent-up emotion whispered, as something knocked her to the ground. Wren stared up horrified into a face that had haunted her nightmares for years -a face twisted with passion and regret and desire.

"Who are you?" she whispered although she feared the answer.

"Need you ask?" a male voice pleaded. "I've been looking for you since before you were born. You are mine! Mine!"

"Don't believe it, Wren," Kyle willed fiercely, internally attuned to what Wren was experiencing, "It's a lie." Kyle felt helpless to intervene physically, as if years rather than mere yards separated them.

"It's no lie," the strained voice responded, even as Wren implored, "Kyle, don't interfere. I can't run anymore."

"Run?" Kyle reflected, "From what?" He glanced about desperately, looking for Mencie to help him but she was nowhere to be seen. Instead the Dean was clawing at his jeans, as if to drag him towards the cabin and away from Wren. Shaking free of the cat, Kyle ran to rescue Wren from the dark shadow bending over her.

"No, Kyle, no," Wren warned, "I have to deal with this myself. No one can help me now." With that, the tenuous thread connecting Kyle to Wren's inner processes snapped.

Baffled, Kyle halted. Wren was in grave danger. Was he to do nothing? Once again, must he stand by as someone he loved more than his own life, entered into a mortal struggle? He stared at Wren's writhing form, unable to decipher what he saw.

Wren grabbed at the clothing of the dark figure pushing

her to the ground but her hand encountered nothing but night air. The form and face hovering over her rippled in the moonlight, swaying like a coiled snake, hypnotic eyes fixed on Wren.

"I know you somehow," Wren stuttered, bewildered by memories that weren't her own. "Who are you? Where have I seen you?"

"Here, Della, here where I've loved you," the wraith hissed. Wren shuddered. She wasn't Della. And yet, at this moment Della was alive in her. And yes, she had visited this murky, shameful place before... these shadowy borderlands where the past relived itself, a past hers and yet not hers. How many nights had she wakened, panicked and sobbing, after such a visit? Wren cringed. A familiar conflict raged through her. Her longing to understand warred with an overwhelming fear of the knowledge she would gain, draining her strength, paralyzing her will.

Kyle, observing the anguish on Wren's face, shook off his own crippling conflicts, and shouted, "Wren! Hang on, I'm coming," though he had no idea how he could reach her or what he could do once he did.

Hearing Kyle's cry breaking the doom that was entrapping her, Wren longed to fling herself into Kyle's protective embrace and bury her face in his shoulder, as she had when wakening from this nightmare in the past. She saw Kyle coming around the heap of rocks and prepared to leap toward him. To run away again... to flee. No! No more running!

"Go back, Kyle. Leave me alone," she protested, and twisted about beneath the dark shape pressing her down. The face that filled Wren's vision seemed suddenly familiar. Tossing up her arms to ward off a kiss, Wren felt herself roughly pinioned against a cold dirt floor. A heavy weight lay over her, penetrating her most feminine regions with hot, repeated thrusts. She gagged and struggled. She was

Della, Della alone in a murky place fighting against a horror that had stalked her for years.

"No!" she shrieked but his weight and passion were too much for her more slender strength. Della was overcome; beaten; defiled, her most intimate sanctuary violated against her will.

"I know now!" Wren choked, a spasm of shame and self-disgust shredding the fragile tissue of her self-respect. A flicker of anxiety lit the wraith's eyes, as if recognition threatened its shadowy existence. Wren went limp, saturated with bitterness and self-loathing. The wraith had to be her uncle...but which one? She couldn't name the full truth but the horror of it spread through her like bile. She was... she was born of incest.

Wren retched, over and over, her stomach rejecting what her mind refused but her heart knew was true. No wonder Della had fled and sought to hide herself and the... the thing she carried! Wren tore at her hair, her clothes, her skin. Someone was grabbing her again, pinioning her arms, clasping her roughly. Wren thrust out blindly, clawing at the strong arms, hissing and spitting until stars shot through her vision and coldness overwhelmed her.

"Wren, Wren, what's wrong?" Kyle's anxious voice penetrated the frigid place where she hid. Warmth seeped into Wren's chilled limbs and she realized Kyle was cradling her in his arms. She clung to him briefly before pushing him away. He mustn't come near her ... no one should! Hysterical laughter erupted from her raw throat. She had found her parents and....

Gently but firmly, Kyle resisted Wren's efforts to free herself from his embrace until racking sobs exhausted her. He had no idea what had terrorized Wren so and she refused his entreaties to tell him.

"I can't even say the word," Wren thought despairingly. "How would Kyle react once he knew what he had married? No! He mustn't find out ... not ever!"

As Wren appeared to relax, Kyle loosened his embrace and she rolled away from him. Seeking to regain her feet, Wren groped for a rock in the cairn behind her. It loosened in her hand, disturbing the entire pile.

"Wren, watch out!" shouted Kyle, leaping up and pulling her with him. "Get out of the way - it's all coming down."

Wren struggled against Kyle's grasp and stumbled just as the heap of boulders and debris collapsed around her. A large stone crashed down on her shin. Wren screamed and blacked out as pain ricocheted through her.

Moans wakened her and she realized they were her own. Kyle was beside her, cursing as he shifted a rock off Wren's leg. Mencie reappeared and assessing the situation, started plucking plantain leaves from the grass about them. Crushing them expertly in her hands, she laid the cool plants on Wren's bruised shin. Gradually the cold tincture numbed the pain and Wren's faintness passed. She sat up.

Avoiding Kyle's worried eyes, Wren focused on the gray figure in the floppy hat. "Are you still here?" she gasped. "Did you see? Do you know ...?"

Mencie's sad, ageless eyes wordlessly answered Wren. "Everything?"

"Yes, I know the whole story."

Anger, despair, confusion raged in Wren's heart. She stared at the stooped, gray figure until Mencie seemed to fade into the mists now rolling into the clearing. Then she heard The Dean pawing at the far side of the tumbled rocks. Hearing the cat's scrabbling, Kyle turned. Curious, he walked around the cairn and then stopped abruptly. "Oh, God," he breathed.

"What is it, Kyle?" Wren called.

When he didn't answer, Wren started to scoot toward him, ignoring her throbbing leg. Mencie's poultice of crushed leaves slipped off.

113

'I'm not sure you want to see this," Kyle replied grimly. Reaching his side, Wren grabbed his hand and pulled herself to her feet. Kyle was staring down at a skeleton still covered with rotted bits of clothing. The cloth was familiar somehow. Where had she seen that print? Oh, no, it... it was in Zettie's album, that last photo of her mother....

Wren leaned heavily against Kyle. "Oh, my God. Oh, my God," she moaned and buried her face against him. Kyle supported Wren until the shudders coursing through her subsided and he could contain his own shock and bewilderment.

"Can you walk?" Kyle asked, and when Wren murmured something about trying, he helped her to a grassy space and eased her to the ground. Replacing the poultice on Wren's shin, Kyle sank down beside her.

"I- I guess we've found Della," Wren observed shakily. "We'll have to tell Zettie."

Kyle nodded while his eyes roamed the glade, searching until he saw Mencie's gray form gliding toward them.

Responding to Kyle's concern Mencie examined Wren's shin more thoroughly. "You're lucky, girl. All you've got is a bad stone bruise. Nothing is broken but you'll have a black and blue leg for a long while. This plantain will ease it and keep some of the swelling down."

"Do you know how Della got here?" Kyle asked Mencie, challenge edging his voice.

"Yes. I know" Mencie replied sadly. "She attempted the long walk back to The Cove too soon after Winnie's birth. She started to hemorrhage badly. I found her and took her into yonder cabin. Della was bitter. I couldn't treat that bitterness and she bled out her spirit. I laid her out as best I could and piled the stones over her body to prevent the beasts from getting to it. But her spirit roams."

Wren struggled to her feet and hobbled about gingerly, restlessly. Mencie roughly pulled Kyle back from helping her.

"Where she walks, you cannot go," she warned, and then disappeared into the pre-dawn twilight spreading through the woods. Wren continued to limp and moan through the glade until finally, she started picking up the stones to rebuild the cairn protecting Della's remains. Silently Kyle began to help her.

CHAPTER ELEVEN

A twig cracked in the shadowy woods and Kyle whirled, catching up a rock as he did so.

"Comin' in," a voice called as Locke's bulky figure emerged from the trees. He carried a basket covered with a cloth. "Maw was up early, fixin' this for you'ns." He gave the mound of stones a passing glance but said nothing.

The fragrance of warm biscuits made Wren realize just how weak she felt. She and Kyle followed Locke around the cabin to where some flat stones lay in the tall grass, now glistening with dew. Out of sight of the rocky cairn, the horrors of the night just past receded slightly.

Unrolling the blanket he had slung across his shoulders, Locke laid out breakfast as the morning brightened. He said little, his face grim. Kyle risked asking how he knew where to find them.

"Mencie told me," Locke allowed shortly.

"Mencie?"

Locke held up his hand. "She met me on the trail."

"I don't trust that one," Kyle muttered.

Locke smiled grimly, "None of us do. She ain't all that safe to be around."

"Yeh, tell me about it! She's more than what she appears," Kyle muttered uneasily.

Locke leaned toward Kyle menacingly, "Don't be astin' me no questions about her. If'n you're meant to know more, she'll tell you."

Wren showed no interest in the men's small talk but took her biscuit and coffee over to a rock on the further edge of the clearing. She stared into the trees, deliberately blocking Locke and Kyle from her line of vision. Kyle noted her rigid stance and kept his distance. When Locke took the thermos over to refill Wren's cup, she flinched visibly.

The piercing whistle of a cardinal sounded from the woods and was echoed from another direction. Locke caught Kyle's sudden alertness.

"That what you heard yesterday over near Bewley's?"

Kyle nodded.

Locke abruptly threw out the last of his coffee. "Got somethin' to tend to," he muttered and disappeared into the underbrush as quietly as a fox.

Kyle glanced toward Wren who was staring blankly ahead, unaware of Locke's sudden departure. A chasm yawned between them that Kyle felt helpless to cross. Wren's features were ashen with fatigue in the cool morning light. Her shallow breathing indicated a state of near shock. Finally Kyle urged Wren to roll up in the blanket and try to sleep. She agreed but when she picked up the blanket and limped toward the cairn with it, Kyle reached out a hand to stop her.

"Not there, Wren, it's not safe," he warned. Wren merely looked at him as if the word 'safe' meant nothing to her now. But she allowed him to lead her back to where the rising sun was beginning to warm the side of the cabin and lay down like a worn out child. Kyle sat beside her, a feeling of helplessness overwhelming him.

Once again he had failed someone he had loved as his

117

other self. Once again, the forces of the spirit world had defeated him. For the first time, as he studied Wren's ravaged features, Kyle bitterly regretted his inability to wield the powers of healer and protector that could have been his. His head dropped to his chest, his hands flexing uselessly in the grass. He may have drowsed for when he opened his eyes, twisting to ease the strain in his back, the sun was full in his face.

Wren slept at Kyle's side, moaning occasionally, her cheeks glistening with tears. She seemed so far away from him now, this wife he cherished; this woman whom he regarded as God's gift to ease his long loneliness. Wren had been a symbol to Kyle of forgiveness and a chance at a new life, a life free of old conflicts. But he had failed her. How had he persuaded himself he could escape the powers that warred within him? "Duped again, Kyle," he mocked.

Restlessly, Kyle pushed to his feet and began pacing the glade. For a while he stayed close, keeping Wren in sight but the brightness of the sun disturbed him. The light made him feel vulnerable, all his secrets open to scrutiny by Powers that had defeated him years before. Without realizing it, Kyle edged further and further into the woods, seeking the deeper shade; a darker glen. In his distraction, Kyle's native skill as a woodsman failed him.

Many disturbed beasts were prowling about, roused by the approaching machinery of the logging crews; their habitat invaded by scouts with guns whose shots ricocheted among the stands of giant trees. Kyle, absorbed in his own inner world of pain and self-recrimination, never even noticed the black hulk squatting by the edge of the path ahead of him until a low growl alerted him. He started, looking up directly into the small, angry eyes of a black bear lumbering to its feet. Two inert bundles of fur lay beside the old sow. The smell of blood and death assaulted Kyle's senses at the same time as the bereaved mother hurled

118

herself at him with astonishing agility.

Instinctively, Kyle leapt backwards into a briar patch that tore his jeans and tripped his feet. The angered beast slashed at the briars with lethal claws missing Kyle by inches. He rolled onto his face, expecting to feel those nails raking his back and teeth gripping his neck at any second. Even in the midst of his terror, Kyle experienced a pang of pity for the demented she-bear. Her grunts and growls climaxed in a high-pitched roar that nearly drowned out a softly-spoken word of command.

"Belva! Quiet! Be still! Back now."

The roar broke off, ending in a single, mournful moan as the great bear lowered her front paws to the ground. She swayed hesitantly, scratching at the thorny branches before turning and lumbering back toward her dead cubs, whimpering softly to herself. Hardly daring to believe himself alive and unscathed, Kyle rolled over and sat up as Mencie approached him through a stand of hemlock.

Her golden eyes gleamed. "That was dumb, Kyle. You know better than to walk up to a bear that's right in your path."

Numbly, Kyle merely nodded, accepting Mencie's scorn as his due.

Not surprisingly, Mencie added, "Follow me, if you please." and began leading Kyle deeper into the woods. Little by little, he grew aware of a difference in the forest. The trees were taller, some with trunks several feet in circumference. More squirrels frisked among their branches than he had ever seen. The ground was liberally marked with paw prints and the gashes of small, sharp hooves. Absently, Kyle identified deer and bobcat;bear and coon. "A hunter's paradise," he mused, his muscles flexing in anticipation of pulling a taut bowstring.

Parting the dense branches of a rhododendron thicket, Mencie stopped. Kyle looked up. Just beyond them, he saw large rocks encircling the base of a towering oak. Looking back over her shoulder, Mencie jerked her head, motioning Kyle into the clearing ahead of her. His eyes widened as he stepped past her. "Grandfather Oak!" he breathed, shivering in awe.

"Go!" Mencie ordered imperiously as Kyle hesitated, torn with both reverence and fear. When he looked back at her, his jaw dropped in amazement. Her gray braids were gone. Glossy black ropes fell gracefully down her back and the beaded band across her forehead proclaimed her status as a faith-keeper of the Cherokee nation. Only the fey golden eyes were the same.

Kyle's feeble resistance wilted under her gaze. Turning from her, he drew a long breath and pushed through the shrubs into the filtered sunlight that danced over the grasses. Mencie followed with a grunt of approval and when Kyle glanced at her again, he saw only the familiar gray gnome he had first encountered on the trail.

She had seated herself on one of the moss-covered boulders and indicated that Kyle do the same. She regarded him closely as he eased himself down reluctantly. "Now, tell me about it," she commanded briskly.

"About Wren? I don't know what's going on with her."

Mencie threw down her gray hat impatiently. "Nor should you until she herself tells you," she retorted. "Tell me what's stopping you from claiming your own heritage... and the powers that should be flowing through you."

Kyle narrowed his eyes, his lips a tight slash across his face. Only the twitching of his jaw muscle betrayed his agitation. He gazed obstinately at the Oak.

"Kyle Makepeace, how much longer are you going to defy the Powers? I brought you here so that you can tell your story to Grandfather Oak." Kyle tugged uselessly when Mencie grabbed his hand and, with remarkable strength, slammed his palm against the bark of the immense tree. The life force in it tingled up Kyle's arm, shattering his resolve.

120

"Tell it!" Mencie ordered.

Moistening his lips, Kyle spoke thickly, painfully. "I haven't spoken Crowe's name aloud since the day he died."

Mencie said nothing. The leaves of the ancient oak rustled sympathetically.

"Crowe. My brother, my twin, three minutes older than I. The only difference between us was that the birthright fell to him. We were never apart, it seemed. And no one could tell us one from the other. Except Ma and Pa, of course. We took each other's place in class; did one another's homework; even traded places on the ball field. We shouldn't have done that. If we hadn't, maybe...." Kyle's voice broke.

"You can't change it now, Kyle," Mencie admonished severely.

"No," he admitted with infinite regret in his voice. "No. But I was the faster runner. If it had been me carrying that football (as everyone thought it was), I might have escaped that tackle and pile up. As it was, Crowe was dragged down by a guy who hated me. He kicked him in the gut and when Crowe doubled up, kicked him in the back. No one saw it because a dozen other guys were on top of them almost at once. Crowe only told me later."

"At first, he just seemed to have some bad bruises but it wasn't long before we knew it was more. His kidneys began bleeding and when the doctors completed their testing, they told us renal failure was inevitable. They could do dialysis for a while until a kidney donor was found."

Kyle took another deep breath. "They didn't have to look far for a match. I was standing right there but I was terrified. I didn't, couldn't say a word when Ma and Pa looked at me that day outside Crowe's room. Actually, no one asked me. Everyone just assumed I was OK and went ahead with the paper work and preparations."

Grandfather Oak

Kyle ran his fingers roughly through his hair and jumped off the rock, pacing around the clearing in anguish. "Just before they put me under to take my kidney, I knew I shouldn't do it... not even for Crowe."

Kyle looked hard at Mencie, taking her measure before continuing. Then addressing the Oak, he said quietly, almost matter of factly, "There was more wrong with Crowe than the doctors realized. But I knew. He and I had always shared body-sense. No matter what they tried, he would die. I fought the medical team and refused to let them take my kidney. When Crowe went into a coma and died a couple days later, everyone blamed me." Kyle reached down and crushed an acorn cap between his fingers. "Pa, I think, was the only one who figured out the whole story."

"Come back here and sit down," Mencie said softly, and once more, gently this time, placed Kyle's hand against Grandfather Oak's rough bark.

When Kyle seemed calm enough, she asked, "So what did your Pa do?"

"He gave me Crowe's birthright."

"Which was?"

Kyle swallowed painfully, "Crowe was to be a shaman. He had already gone on his vision quest and been received by the spirits."

"He was very young for that," Mencie murmured doubtfully.

"Perhaps," Kyle acknowledged, "perhaps he knew he didn't have much time to fulfill his destiny. It was the only time we were ever apart physically."

"Were you apart?" Mencie inquired.

Kyle sighed again. "No, not really. He was off by himself on the mountain but I shared in everything that happened there. We even talked about it later, trying to figure out the parts we didn't understand."

"What didn't you understand?"

Kyle smiled grimly. "The mantle never quite touched him; never rested on his shoulders. It seemed to be waiting for something more."

"Or someone else?" Mencie suggested softly.

Kyle shrugged. "It wasn't meant for me. I was already destined for the priesthood."

"What did you do?"

"Do?"

"When your Pa wanted you to take up the mantle."

"I walked out ... and never saw him again. There was a fire that night and my folks didn't get out. They died of smoke inhalation in their bed."

"And you?"

'My only home then was the seminary school where Crowe and I had been studying. I went back and decided to become a priest - to seize that kind of power instead and use it against him."

"Him?"

"God," Kyle said flatly.

Mencie gasped sharply. "Fool!" she hissed. "No wonder the barriers are being breached."

Before Kyle could stop her, Mencie grasped the front of his shirt and ripped it open, revealing the pouch that hung around his neck. She studied the markings on it intently and then nodded to herself. "I see why Belva went for you. I should have let her mark you, scion of the Bear."

Kyle sucked in his breath and pulled away from Mencie. "I have been marked," he muttered.

"Show me!"

Kyle tugged off his right boot to reveal a deeply scarred foot. "I told Wren I'd stepped into a trap while out hunting with my father."

"What really happened?"

"Crowe and I were out hunting with our Pa when we were nine. A rabid bear broke into our camp and caught me by the heel as I tried to climb up a tree behind Crowe. Pa shot it and rushed me off to the hospital. I had to go through the whole rabies treatment and nearly lost my foot when infection set in. But Pa wouldn't let them take it off and vowed that I would not only walk on it but run as well."

Kyle gave a short laugh. "That's why I could run faster than Crowe. Pa made him race me until I got so mad that I stopped favoring my foot and just flat out beat him."

"Yes, I see now," Mencie mused. "It was meant to be so." She was silent for a few minutes before levering herself off the rock. "Come along, Kyle, you and Belva need one another."

Too exhausted to demand further explanation, Kyle complied, plodding behind Mencie as she led him back to the briar patch. The old sow was still there, crouched down by the bodies of her twin cubs, prodding first one, than the other still form. She licked their eyes, driving off the flies that were gathering. Her whimpers were tinged with despair now rather than anger, and pity for her penetrated Kyle's benumbed spirit.

Mencie reached up and placing her hand on Kyle's shoulder, pressed him down to the ground until he was on all fours. From this angle, Belva appeared immense to Kyle. What also came into view were the swollen teats that she vainly tried to get the cubs to suckle. Mencie stared hard at Kyle, a command in her golden eyes. "Accept the mantle, Kyle Makepeace," she said, "or be responsible for more deaths."

The final threads of Kyle's resistance unraveled and he laid his face against the earth. "Mother," he breathed, "Mother, give me your strength. If I die now, let it be while trying to accept what I have run from all my life." Deliberately, Kyle pulled open the pouch that hung from his neck and scattered a libation of the powder on the earth.

Then he crept out from under the briars and toward the

mourning bear. Her head came up and they locked gazes. Kyle's nostrils twitched as he inhaled her rank odor mingling with the smell of death emanating from the cubs. Slowly, staring at Belva with profound compassion and reverence, Kyle crept closer until he almost touched one of the cubs. He paused. When Belva made no move, Kyle eased himself flat onto the ground beside the bundle of black fur and waited.

As if losing interest in him, Belva returned to her keening, turning over the baby closest to her. When it did not respond, she shifted her weight and reached toward the other cub. Her claw grazed Kyle's shirt where he lay curled round himself, trying to control the spasms of fear racing through him. She stopped, startled by the body heat she detected and for a moment, something like hope lit her small eyes. She pushed Kyle gently. He forced himself to remain totally still, wholly vulnerable, as her nose investigated the hair on his head.

Belva grunted, baffled by the strange odor mixing with that of her cub. When Kyle didn't flinch, the sow opened her mouth and tentatively licked his ear. Tickled by her tongue, Kyle shook his head and she retreated suspiciously.

"Belva," Kyle murmured soothingly and held out his fingers, still dusted by the powder from his pouch. Delicately she sniffed his proffered hand and when she made no aggressive moves, Kyle risked curling up and onto his knees. He crawled across the still body of the cub and approached the bear who was now rocking slowly back and forth on her haunches.

Kyle struggled for control. What was required of him wholly contradicted his image of how to obtain the blessing of a totemic god. Everything in him cringed as his senses were assaulted by the stench of the coarse-haired creature before him. Forcing himself to move with utmost gentleness now, Kyle gave in to the implacable force guiding him and put his lips around one of Belva's teats, sucking in the warm milk.

The sow sighed and laid back, allowing him to massage her tender teats and relieve their pressure. The milk spurted out, splashing Kyle's face. The old bear's maternal warmth surrounded him, easing away the turmoil and pain of his lifelong conflict. Kyle surrendered, closed his eyes and suckled. A distant part of him wondered why he was not being torn apart. To be given milk rather than have blood taken....

The great bear relaxed and without lifting his head, Kyle could hear a contented rumbling deep within her. Slowly he rubbed some of the powder from his pouch onto the sow's teats where the suckling cubs had worn the fur away. Belva rested, appearing to sleep. Kyle watched the massive breast rising and falling, mesmerized by the rhythm until he himself began rocking in unison with it.

The massive body began to shimmer before his eyes and another bear seemed to rise from it, large and luminous in the shadowy glen. Kyle bowed low and the great paws came to rest around his head. Power flowed into Kyle, electrifying his entire frame. He felt suffused with heat as a reservoir of energy gushed up from his depths. Kyle shuddered and moaned, experiencing a liberation of the powers he had so long suppressed. The luminous bear figure enveloped him but instead of feeling smothered, Kyle felt invigorated as this mighty spirit mingled with his own soul. Once more Kyle prostrated himself on the breast of Mother Earth, surrendering totally to powers far greater than his by right.

CHAPTER TWELVE

How long he lay there, Kyle didn't know. When he once more became aware of his surroundings, the sun was directly overhead. He sat up abruptly. Something was different. Belva was gone but the two dead cubs still lay near him, one on either side. Kyle slowly rose to his feet. His jeans and shirt were torn but his body felt remarkably whole and strong. He flexed his hands, momentarily surprised not to behold claws at his fingertips.

Kyle brushed his hair out of his eyes and retied the twisted kerchief that held it in place. There were things he had to do. He searched for a stout branch and with it hollowed out a shallow grave in the soft ground beyond the briar patch. As he picked up the bodies of the cubs, Kyle studied the shotgun wounds that had killed them from almost point-blank range. Their deaths had been deliberate and wanton destruction. In his heart, Kyle knew they had died so that he might live. He owed it to them, his bear brothers, to accept the medicine powers of the bear spirit, even as he owed it to his twin, Crowe, to don the mantle of the shaman that had fallen to him.

Reverently, Kyle buried the small bodies and scattered leaves over the fresh earth. Then he turned and trotted swiftly back up the trail to where he had left Wren.

Kyle found her huddled in the shadow of the Waitsel cabin stroking the soft gray fur of The Dean who curled beside her. Wren's hair hung limply about her face, the normally bouncy curls flattened and tangled. When Kyle greeted her, Wren turned toward him with a listless, unfocused gaze. Kyle, looking into her eyes, briefly glimpsed an abyss of horror that shook him. Stirred with compassion, he bent over to kiss Wren but she turned her head sharply and his lips merely grazed her hair.

Thoughtfully, hopefully, he stroked her hair and waited for the power within him to radiate warmth and healing. But no such thing happened. Instead, Wren merely got up and limped away from him. Baffled, Kyle followed her as she resumed her agonized pacing of the clearing that enclosed Della's grave and the Waitsel cabin. Wren's inner conflict was so bitter that she effectively shut out any help Kyle could give. This grieved him, for of all people he longed to heal, Wren was first and foremost.

Instinctively, Kyle did the one thing that kept Wren from driving him away entirely. He remained silent and merely walked with her, round and round the glade. When she tired and sat on the ground hugging her knees and rocking back and forth, Kyle kept time with her. After a while, this silent syntony that asked nothing but to be with her appeared to soothe Wren. Some color returned to her face and vigor to her movements.

She allowed Kyle to help her finish rebuilding the pile of rocks over Della's grave and as they did so Kyle noticed they were a collection of remarkably beautiful stones. Obviously someone had brought specially chosen rocks to the cairn over the years, someone who also knew where Della's body lay. Mencie would not have felt this need to beautify the spot and Locke appeared far too bitter to bother. Who was this unknown person? Absorbed in his reflections, Kyle was startled when Wren broke her silence to ask, "Where did we leave our gear, Kyle?"

He paused, trying to remember back to what seemed another lifetime, though it was less than twenty-four hours ago.

"At Zettie's, your Mamaw's," he finally said.

Wren grimaced. "I don't want to go back there now. How can I face her?" she muttered. "But...." She sighed.

Kyle took advantage of her unspoken request for help. "Wren, dear, you don't have to tell me anything. I understand that you can't. But perhaps you would accept something that may help you to carry this burden?"

Wren leapt back like a skittish doe but Kyle took hope because she kept her blue-green eyes fastened on him. "Sit here on the blanket," he directed, and felt encouraged when she complied. Silently invoking the spirit of heart's ease, Kyle knelt beside her. He didn't touch Wren but just slid his hands gently over and down the aura of deep pain in which she was immersed, crooning soft words that Crowe had learned long before and which were now his to use. Slowly Wren relaxed and some of the tension in her body diminished even as tears ran silently down her face.

At last Wren stirred and whispered, "That ... whatever you've done ... has helped me. I think I can go back to Zettie's with you now and get our stuff." She squinted up at the sun. "Maybe we'll have time to get out of The Cove before dark if we hurry."

Privately Kyle doubted that Zettie would allow Wren to leave The Cove in the state she was in but he judged Wren's composure too fragile to argue with her. Best leave that to Zettie! Silently, he picked up the blanket and basket and prepared to lead the way back toward Zettie's. By the time they reached the little house in The Cove, Wren might have recovered some of her natural resilience. They set out through woods that whispered uneasily. Again, Kyle was struck with the absence of the normal sounds of life about them. It was as if the forest knew of an impending threat and had sent all its more vulnerable inhabitants into hiding. Even the trees seemed to be gripping the soil more firmly.

The silent walk through the forest had some restorative effect on Wren, for when they came in sight of Zettie rocking on her front porch, Wren was able to wave and call out to her with some semblance of her former energy. Zettie jumped up and ran out to meet them, embracing Wren before she could push her away. If Wren's lack of response to her hug puzzled Zettie, the older woman gave no sign of it.

Zettie looked up and welcomed Kyle, adding, "Locke is in the house. He just got back a few minutes ago and looks wore out. He and Mencie have had a very busy day - there were far more scouts in the woods than they had reckoned with."

Leaving Wren to explain that they had just returned for their camping gear and were intending to depart The Cove before dark, Kyle strode into the kitchen where he found Locke splashing cold water on his face and hair.

"Rough day?" Kyle inquired.

Locke shook drops from his head and grunted, "Yep. They shouldn't have been able to come in so far. T'aint good."

Kyle clenched his fist, his mistrust of Locke deepening. Surly and short on words, there was something secretive about this bulky farmer with his sharp, narrow eyes.

Throwing down the towel, Locke continued, "The scouts struck in as far as the Bentley homestead before getting all turned around."

"All turned around?"

"Yeah, Mencie did her thing and before these guys realized it, they were halfway across the trestle bridge. In the thick fog and all, they almost ran right off where the mid-section is collapsed. She left them climbing down the scaffolding into the gorge. They din't care to return."

Kyle raised his eyebrows.

"You've heard tell of the bears on Unaka Mountain, ain't you?" Locke asked, a cunning gleam in his eye. "Welp, seems as how some big'uns was on these fellers' tail-feathers by the time they reached the bridge. Guys appeared to judge it best to jest keep movin' on."

"Yeah.' Kyle admitted carefully, watching Locke pour some tea water from Zettie's ever-ready kettle. He didn't want to pursue the subject of Mencie vis-a-vis bears with anyone, least of all, Locke.

Kyle was reaching for a cup when it struck him. "What do you mean, the middle section of the trestle is collapsed? Wren and I crossed over it when we came in."

"You did? You'ns was lucky then," Locke allowed.

Before Kyle could digest the import of Locke's remark. Wren and Zettie scurried into the kitchen. "Porter just sent word through Jonah," Zettie told the men. "The Forest Service is fixin' to punch the loggin' road through startin' tomorrow. Fact is, they've got dozers almost up to the Borderlands right now. Oma's callin' everyone over to her place this evenin' so we can get started settin' up the barriers."

"Why start so early? Nobody's goin' to be movin' afore day- light, are they?" Locke countered sourly.

"Oma's not so sure. Neither am I." Zettie paused and sighed. "We might have to deal with a 'gate' we don't know about. Best get everyone there and see if it shows up."

Kyle shot a mystified glance at Wren who was scrutinizing Zettie. "Just what do you mean by a 'Gate', Mamaw?"

Zettie paused as she donned her apron. "Someone has weakened the Barriers. You'ns will understand before this night is over, Winnie."

"We won't be here, Mamaw," Wren began but the busy little lady just waved her hand at her. "Hesh, now. You'ns are needed, both of you. Git to holpin' me now."

132

With a shrug of defeat, Wren joined Zettie who began bustling about preparing food to take to an all-night vigil. Locke rustled up jugs and bottles to fill with sweetened iced tea while Kyle was sent out to pluck lettuce from the garden. Wren found herself working on a tray of deviled eggs. Deftly Zettie mixed flour, shortening and water, patting it into biscuits that she popped into the hot oven pan after pan.

Despite their haste, a serenity pervaded the kitchen that soothed Wren's tormented spirit. Tenderness emanated from Zettie and Wren knew she was praying. She writhed inwardly, beset by her fear that Zettie might penetrate her dark secret. Suddenly Zettie turned to her.

"Spit it out, child. Tell me what you found out about Della." Wren stiffened defensively, her hands slowing as she considered how much she dare reveal. She licked her lips as she turned sad eyes toward Zettie. "We found Della's body at the Waitsel cabin," she began. "Mencie had buried her there, oh, years ago. Not long after I was born, I guess."

Zettie listened silently, her face a mask of grief. As Wren's voice petered out, she gave the younger woman a sharp look.

"There's more happened than you're tellin' me, child," she began, but then stopped suddenly when Locke crashed so noisily through the door with baskets and tote bags that Wren wondered if he had been listening from outside. Her stomach knotted convulsively as he brushed past her.

Under Zettie's brisk direction, they packed up the food and set out toward Oma's under a lavender evening sky. Some dark shapes were skirting the woods and Kyle twitched nervously. It was one thing to hear red wolves howling at a distance; another to see their rusty-gray forms silently patrolling the near edge of the meadow. Perhaps it was better that he and Wren were not leaving just yet. Locke strode on ahead, swinging his head this way and that, sniffing the air like a suspicious bear.

133

Once more Wren and Kyle found themselves at a gathering of The Cove community, this time in Oma's hospitable kitchen. As Wren put her tray on a long table already laden with food, she noted a pail of strawberries. From Bewley and Haidia, no doubt. The old couple was chatting with Jonah who held a paper in his hand. He waved Kyle and Wren over to where he stood in the fading light from the bay window. The round table was covered with roughly drawn maps.

"This email came in just a bit ago - another message from Porter," Jonah rumbled. "A hunting buddy of his told him more about the scouts the Forest Service is using. The Waitsel boys are among them. Seems the Service believes their story about a bunch of folks living back here. It don't make sense that those boys would've said anything about The Cove even if their own kin don't come back here no more. But Porter would know, I guess. He seemed mighty certain that the feds are looking for The Cove. If'n they find us, they'll turn us out. They don't want anyone on government land especially now that it's opened up to logging."

Locke, who had joined them, frowned. "Ne'er liked Sarie and Zach Waitsel. Trashed that place they had afore they moved on. I had no truck with 'em. Maw said she was worried about a 'gate.' Could be it's their boys. They probably know just enough from their folks to be used by the spirits in the borderland."

Locke caught Zettie's eye and motioned her over with his chin. After hearing Porter's latest report, Zettie's eyes darkened with concern. "Somethin's not fittin' together here and my Sight is blocked." Zettie's gnarled hands trembled as she brushed invisible stains from her apron. "Might be a right busy night," she observed with a sigh.

Just then, Oma called everyone into the front parlor that ran the length of the house. A fieldstone fireplace dominated one end; a sunroom, silhouetted in the mauve twilight enclosed the opposite end. Between them, a low-beamed ceiling stretched over book-lined walls and scattered furniture.

Chatter subsided as folks entered the room. Kyle had never seen an endangered group so serene. No one appeared to be in charge and for a long while people sat silently on chairs, stools or propped against the walls, relaxed but expectant. And breathing. Kyle and Wren had chosen an old settee where they leaned back, shoulders barely touching. Wren clasped her hands tightly in her lap; Kyle's arms crossed his chest.

Soon Kyle noticed both he and Wren had begun breathing in unison with everyone else in the room. The stillness was profound. The only light emanated from the pyramid of candles Oma had lit on the mantel piece. Wren became keenly aware of Centers of Power strategically situated about the room. Without turning her head, she identified Zettie, Oma, Jonah, and some of the other leaders from the previous night's assembly wielding a force that focused the group. On the perimeter of her inner vision, Wren detected Mencie roaming about like a sheep dog, keeping the flock together and alert for menaces in the night.

Occasionally the breeze moaning down the chimney carried the howling of wolves, now near, now far. The energy generated by people totally given to the one task of protecting The Cove translated itself into ghostly sounds, a whispering of distant panpipes; a faint shivering of breaking glass. The windows of the room turned opaque as a heavy mist licked its way through The Cove, muffling everything in thick whiteness. Zettie's voice was so muted that Kyle and Wren didn't note precisely when she began speaking from her place in the sunroom.

"...and so there is one among us who is betraying their own," she disclosed sadly. "We don't know who it is and he or she may not even realize they have become a gateway... let us all pray for one another."

A dart of anxiety pierced the prayerfulness of the group. The room rustled as people stirred uneasily, no one daring to look even at their nearest neighbor. One among them? Here? Tonight?

Wren stiffened and Kyle felt the back of his neck prickle. Some power larger than themselves directed them to focus on the burning triangle. It subtly changed hues, fading from red-orange to blue-green. As the steady glow began to dim, Wren squeezed her hands together painfully. Words echoed softly through the room: "One among us will betray us." Sweat beaded her upper lip. Was it she?

CHAPTER THIRTEEN

Zettie, watching from her vantage point at the back of the group, felt a heaviness invade her spirit. One of her neighbors or relatives had become a gateway for powers bent on destroying The Cove. This had never happened in her lifetime and she felt a grave responsibility in the matter. Had she failed the group in some way? As a Guardian of The Cove, should she have detected this sooner? She had been so preoccupied in her joy over Winnie's arrival that she had not given sufficient attention to the unease and confusion afflicting various Cove members, a state that in the past, had signaled a breach in the barriers. Why had she failed to note a gate swinging open to admit intruders? Could her blind-ness be an effect of the breach or was she herself the unwitting Gate?

Zettie's gnarled fingers quivered in her lap, her heart twist- ing in unaccustomed self-accusation. Reluctantly she admitted that she had not focused on the meaning of events around her because she had feared confirmation of a deeply buried suspicion. The discovery of Winnie Lovada, Della's child, had wakened long suppressed apprehensions about her only daughter and her sons. Zettie's eyes burned with unshed tears and only when she shifted to extract a handkerchief from her dress pocket did she notice a hulking shadow approaching her. Jonah knelt by Zettie's stooped figure, his eyes on a level with hers. "Is it I, Zettie?" he asked, his shoulders hunched anxiously.

"Why do you ask?"

"There's things I haven't told you; things that didn't seem important at the time," Jonah whispered with shame. 'We have so many powers at our disposal - no one knows that better than you, Zettie. I felt sure we could withstand any assault, human or otherwise. I failed to consider how much depends on our mutual trust of one another."

Zettie silently put her hand on Jonah's arm, prompting him to continue. "There's things I know about some folks who have recently arrived."

Looking deep into Zettie's anxious eyes, Jonah nodded. "Yes, it has to do with Wren and Kyle."

Zettie longed to cover her ears and block out hearing from another what her heart had already intuited. But Jonah bowed his head and continued his confession, confiding all he knew of Kyle's background. The gambling with God that had marked Kyle's life disturbed Zettie but the focus of her concern was elsewhere.

"What do you know of Wren?" she whispered through dry lips.

"Very little," Jonah admitted. "But I suspect that Locke and Porter know more than they've told you."

Zettie's heart contracted as she realized that events set in motion years earlier were moving inexorably toward their final (and possibly catastrophic) conclusion. "I've been a fool," she berated herself. "Is The Cove to be lost because of my blindness?"

Zettie was jerked from her bitter thoughts by Jonah's warm hands grasping hers, his eyes beseeching a forgiveness she could not give herself. She smiled grimly, "Jonah, you are not the only one at fault here. I've fallen down, too, and The Cove is paying the price. The betrayer we are dealing with this night does not stand alone in his or her guilt. Let us pray ... that we can bear ... and survive the trial ahead."

Jonah squeezed Zettie's hands and heaved himself to his feet. As he did so, a gray figure fluttered into the sunroom, alighting noiselessly as a bat. Mencie peered through the gloom at Zettie. "It's my fault. It's all my fault," she moaned, her wizened features more gargoyle-like than ever.

Zettie said nothing. Mencie had given more than one lifetime to guarding The Cove. It was inconceivable that she could now, even inadvertently, have betrayed them.

"Mencie, Mencie," Zettie crooned, taking her old friend's hands in hers. "What do you mean?"

"Many years ago something happened in the borderlands," Mencie whispered in anguish. "I literally buried the evidence."

Zettie scrunched Mencie's bony fingers fiercely, "Winne told me about Della, Mencie, but she didn't tell me everything, did she? What do you know? Why haven't you said anything before this?"

"I daren't tell you, Zettie. What I know is only a suspicion - a hunch about something so unspeakable that I couldn't burden you with my uncertain guess."

Zettie's stomach lurched as many vague clues coalesced into a horrible certainty. "No!" she whimpered, "Not that. Not when I've just found Winnie Lovada."

Mencie gazed with immense sympathy at her old friend's anguish. She knew Zettie had finally divined Della's secret and it was near to killing her.

Mencie beat her hands on her head. "Why didn't I say something sooner, Zettie? I thought my vigilance could ward off the consequences and no one need ever know...." she choked and her mouth worked silently. Finally, fiercely, she burst out, "I've become soft in the head from having

139

too much power and knowledge. Take it from me, Zettie, before I misuse it even more. I am dangerous. Perhaps it's my silence that has opened the door!"

Zettie pulled Mencie to herself. "Perhaps it has. Mencie dear. I can't take the burden of your power from you nor tell you how to use it. But I can tell you this. You are not alone in allowing the evil we face this night."

Zettie leaned back in her chair, eyes closed, tired beyond telling. Memories and suspicions she had long suppressed were breaking her heart and she was powerless to prevent them. Black waters of anxiety swept through her. Doubt gnawed at her. Perhaps it was the end of The Cove? Caused by cowardice (and more) on her part?

Zettie groped for a mooring post and her fingers brushed something warm and soft that had leapt into her lap. She opened her eyes to find The Dean regarding her solemnly. Giving her a slight nod, he proceeded to arrange himself on her knees, ears perked forward. Zettie stroked his silken body absently until she felt someone touch her shoulder.

"Is it I, Maw?" Locke whispered anxiously. Zettie sucked in her breath and the Dean stopped purring.

She frowned as she patted the hand of her older son and forced herself to respond calmly, "Search your own heart, Locke. Is there something you are hiding from me? I see only darkness when I pray for our family and I fear that we are deeply involved in this betrayal. What do you know about this?"

Locke stared sadly at Zettie. His mouth twitched anxiously but no words came. He shook his head despairingly and slowly turned aside, lumbering from her sight. Zettie's heart twisted savagely. "Do what you must, my son," she whispered hopelessly as Locke slipped out into the night.

Zettie was stroking the Dean's throat when someone dropped heavily onto a chair beside her.

A fragrance of wood smoke and onions announced Oma's presence. That lady nervously smoothed her hands over her wiry gray hair, brushed at a spot on her bib overalls, and finally folded her arms over her ample breasts, rocking back and forth until the chair creaked in protest.

"Oma?" Zettie murmured.

"Ah'm afraid, Zettie, Ah'm afraid it's me that is allowing this trouble to come to us."

"How so?"

"I love The Cove too much. I can't stand the idea that anything but good ever happens here. I set my mind against it."

"Oma!" Zettie responded in alarm. "What be youn's talkin' about?"

"Anson Jack and me found out somethin' years back, somethin' so bad that we vowed to never tell," she smothered her face in her hands as Anson stepped awkwardly out of the shadows. "We was out huntin' 'sang, he said, "and came upon a patch of it in the clearin' round the Waitsel place. There was a stench in the air, old but unmistakable... we, we looked under the heap of rocks behind the cabin... jest couldn't bring ourselves to tell you and Clyde," he ended forlornly.

Zettie's chin dropped to her chest. How many others had known all along? But what was it that decided Oma and Anson Jack to keep silent about what they had stumbled across? Zettie's lips framed the question but she couldn't bring herself to ask it.

"Zettie, we was wrong to hide what we found," Anson Jack broke in hoarsely, "... but we figured on the boy tellin' you. There was fresh flowers laid there and we'd kotched sight of him...." Oma jerked nervously and Anson Jack's voice faltered. He kneaded his wife's shoulders as he leaned forward, his face drawn and pale under his sunburn. "Our silence warn't fair to you and Clyde but it was like they was powers there too strong for us and now, now we're afeared they're loose within the barriers."

Zettie's white hair began to rise on her scalp. She shuddered. "Oma! Anson Jack! Wild dogs have crept into this sheepfold! How have we all been so blind, so unwilling to track down and face up to the truth of what has happened?"

Oma threw out her work-roughened hands. "It was too horrible to face, Zettie. Nothin' like that should happen among Cove members. We thought maybe silence and time would allow for a cure. But mostly we was jest afeared! We aided this hateful thing by saying nothin'. You see," she pleaded, "we couldn't bear to see the good here all muddied by one of our'n...." She dropped her hands despairingly and leaned back against Anson's bony frame.

Zettie lifted her head, "Listen!"

Anguished whispers drifted throughout the room as various persons moved about in the shadows, approaching other Guardians of The Cove with their individual burdens of guilt. The harmony of the praying community was marked by dissonances. But even as they listened, the broken melodies resolved themselves and formed new harmonies composed of acceptance and forgiveness. Life was stirring in The Cove as members shed complacency, shaken by a threat no one imagined could touch them.

Wren had felt her focus frazzling as people in the room began to stir. Since Zettie's announcement, she had hunched numbly in her place, unconsciously widening the space between herself and Kyle. Unable to sit still any longer, her fear that she herself might be the Gate torturing her, Wren finally wandered into the kitchen. The broad room, with its lingering odors of bacon frying, bread baking and onions cooking brought her a measure of distracted comfort. Cove members stood about in small clusters, drinking tea or munching items from the counter, murmuring uneasily.

Jonah and Zettie soon followed Wren into the kitchen, their faces drawn. She watched curiously as they spoke briefly with various individuals in the room who blanched, glanced her way, and then departed swiftly. Wren picked up a mug and walked over to the wood stove where a large enamel coffeepot was warming. Her hands quivering, Wren splashed the coffee as she attempted to pour it. Kyle, who had entered the kitchen shortly after Wren, came up beside her with a frayed rag. He was about to ask Wren if she were burnt when he saw her flinch. Zettie had suddenly crossed the room and seized Wren's arm.

Without preamble, she ordered, "There's a chore for you this night, child. Only you can close the gate in the barrier to the Borderlands."

"Me?" Wren squeaked. She felt Kyle move closer to her protectively.

"We have no idea what this is all about," Kyle demanded roughly. "How can we do what you and the others cannot?"

Zettie made no response to Kyle's challenge. Wren studied her ashen features and her own heart sickened. "This Gate," Wren began, her lips dry and trembling, "What do you mean by that term? What can you tell me? Is it ... is it a person? Someone you know? M-m-me?"

Zettie turned her face aside. "I can't answer that."

Kyle glared at Zettie. "You mean, you *won't* answer that." The beaten look Zettie turned on him undercut Kyle's anger. He knew she doted on her family and suspected she was protecting someone. But how could she send Wren out as a scapegoat? Kyle's anger flared anew.

Beneath the hubbub of voices in the increasingly crowded kitchen, Zettie reiterated softly but fiercely, "Winnie, only you can save The Cove."

Wren turned back towards the stove, taut with anguish and trembling with fear. Then her shoulders slumped.

143

"What does it matter if I die," she mumbled to herself. "I shouldn't be alive in the first place. Perhaps once I'm gone, The Cove will be purged." Kyle didn't catch all her words but her tone of despair disturbed him profoundly.

Relentlessly Zettie continued, "Winnie Lovada, you have powers you do not yet understand."

"Powers?" Wren echoed bitterly. "How can you say that?" "Because you are your mother's daughter."

Zettie forced Wren about and bringing her face close to Wren's, glared fiercely into her eyes.

Stung, Wren flung back, "Yes, and who else's?"

Zettie did not answer but her face crumpled in agony.

Kyle watched the exchange anxiously. A lot more was going on here than he knew. He wanted to comfort Wren but she had withdrawn again beyond the mysterious chasm that had opened between them the night they'd found Della's body. Wren stood so still and vulnerable she reminded Kyle of a mortally wounded doe. What could he do?

Jonah joined the little group by the stove. His bulk partially blocked the light from the flickering lanterns hanging from ceiling hooks. Accurately assessing the situation, he rumbled at Kyle, "Leave it, son. Wren has a mission only she can fulfill."

Stubbornly Kyle shook his head but when Wren herself pulled away from him, he felt defeated. Zettie, her face bleak, gently took Wren's elbow and guided the younger woman toward the back door. Firmly she propelled Wren across the threshold and into the dark, swirling mists outside. Kyle glared once at Jonah and strode defiantly through the door after Wren.

In the shrouded stillness, Zettie whispered brokenly, "Go with God, my daughter." Turning blindly, she re-entered the kitchen, shutting the door behind her. Sagging against Jonah's bulk, she moaned, "What have I done?"

"All you can, Zettie, all you can," he whispered gently. "Wren doesn't go out unprotected. You've sent out the best we have to ward and guard her. Many unknown to her are watching throughout the Cove this night."

CHAPTER FOURTEEN

Moonlight heightened the smothering density of the fog pressing down on Kyle and Wren as they stumbled down the porch steps. By the time they reached the front gate of Oma's yard, the house itself was all but invisible. Wren jumped, startled by the sound of boots crunching the gravel track beyond her limited range of vision. She whirled around to confront a tall figure emerging from the mists.

"Uncle Porter?" she asked uncertainly. "I ... we didn't know you were in The Cove."

"I had to come back, Winnie. This danger is ... well, too grave for you to deal with alone. Besides," he asked ominously, "Where's Locke?"

His tone reinforced Wren's silent loathing of the sullen tobacco farmer who always turned up where least expected. Did Porter suspect Locke was somehow involved in the present threat to The Cove? Had he come back planning to stop him? Wren wondered if Porter knew about her own heart-sickening suspicions of his brother. Gratitude for this unexpected help from an ally lifted her spirits. For the first time that evening, Wren experienced an upsurge of hope.

She glanced toward Kyle expecting him to reflect her

rising hope. Instead she was disturbed to see him studying Porter with critical intensity. Did he not trust Porter? Or any of the Cove people, for that matter? Could she trust Kyle now? Distressed by her conflicting reactions, Wren's anger flared. Before she could chide Kyle, Porter broke in sharply, "I heard from my buddies just where the forest service plans to punch the road through. Could be that's where the Barriers are weakened."

"Mamaw sent me out to 'save the Cove,' Uncle Porter," Wren's voice was sharp with frustration. "But I have no idea how she expects me to do that....."

When Porter said nothing, she added, "Mamaw said I have... that I have 'powers.' What could she mean by that?"

Porter's breath hissed slightly and he narrowed his eyes, appraising Wren. Kyle noted a flicker of fear pass over his smooth features. Before Kyle could say anything to Wren, Porter spoke briskly.

"Maw usually knows what she's about. How about I take you to where I suspect the Barriers have weakened? Could be that's where you ought to start, Winnie."

"What do folks mean by The Barriers, Uncle Porter?" Wren queried.

"You'll know soon enough, Winnie," Porter responded brusquely before turning to Kyle. "We don't want to be followed, you understand?" Kyle didn't but he listened without comment as Porter went on. "We don't know where Locke is, do we? I've a suspicion he might be out ahead of us, going toward the Bentley Place. You know how to get there from here?"

Kyle nodded, his chin indicating the road leading past the Garenflo brothers' cabin.

"Good. Use that track. Winnie and I will circle around by the old path and meet you there in the clearing. The logging road is coming through right near there."

The Waitsel Place with Della's Cairn

Kyle wavered, reluctant to leave Wren, even with her uncle.

But knowing Wren's resentment of any questions about her newly discovered family, Kyle said nothing. Against his better judgment, he turned down the road. "If you meet up with Locke," Porter warned, "don't tell him I'm here. Head him away from the Bentley place. Best go with him, if you can. No need for him to know where Winnie is either," Porter added with peculiar emphasis.

Wren stumbled as she turned to follow her uncle and when Porter grabbed the top of her sweat shirt to steady her, his thumb hooked the chain around her neck. Instinctively, Wren jerked back and the chain snapped. The disk tinkled on the gravel. Wren groped for it but Porter was quicker. He flashed his light on it and drew in a sharp breath.

"Where did you get this?"

"I-I've always had it," Wren responded puzzled. "I think it once belonged to my mother." For some reason she didn't understand, Wren hesitated to mention that an unnamed man had delivered it to her foster-mother for her when she was an infant.

Porter nodded, slowly caressing the dull metal. "You won't need this tonight as much as I will, girl," he said softly. "May I ....? just for a while?"

Wren looked up at him, puzzled, "Why would you need it, Uncle Porter?"

"It has a rendezvous with the one who once wore it," he replied, a strange smile playing briefly across his lean features.

"Will that help close this Gate that Mamaw talks about?" Wren asked.

"Might could," Porter responded. He closed his long fingers around the disk with a grunt of satisfaction and dropped it into his pocket. Wren felt herself oddly vulnerable without the comforting weight of the pendant between her breasts.

"Grab my belt," Porter commanded."We have some rough ground to travel. I know how to avoid the worst of it so stay close on my heels." Porter set off so quickly that Wren was soon breathless, struggling to keep her hold on him in the dark. Her nagging distress over the absence of the disk was soon erased by her more immediate concern with maintaining her footing. But the haunting sensation of defenselessness returned as Porter dragged her deeper into an unfamiliar part of the woods surrounding The Cove.

Kyle, meanwhile, had set off in the opposite direction, his unease with Porter's sudden appearance replaced by the anger that Zettie and Wren's final exchange had aroused. Absorbed in his jumbled emotions, Kyle made no effort to disguise the crunching of his booted feet on the Cove road. He didn't hear stealthy steps following him through the fog until he broke through the underbrush into the clearing around the remains of the Bentley cabin.

He nearly leapt out of his skin when a harsh whisper asked, "Where's Winnie? Ain't she with you?" Kyle reached for his knife as he whirled and ducked, only to find his sheath empty. A grim chuckle emerged from the mists. "And you consider yourself a woodsman!"

"Locke?" Kyle rasped, anxiety coursing through him. "That you?"

"Who were you 'spectin?" responded the bulky figure closing in on Kyle. "I ast you. Where's Winnie?"

"Not sure," Kyle hedged.

"What you mean by that? Where'd you leave her at?"

"I left her at Oma's place," Kyle said as he backed away from Locke. He knew now that Locke had somehow lifted his knife from his belt as he had approached the clearing. That being so, the advantage was all in the hands of Wren's uncle who Kyle felt little reason to trust.

"'Spect she's still there?"

"I doubt it," Kyle responded. "Zettie sent her out to find 'The Gate' but what that means and why, I'm clueless."

Locke's shrewd face tightened in the pale moonlight that illumined the clearing. "Maw may have finally figured out what all's happened." he muttered more to himself than to Kyle. "How else would she know only Winnie could do it... what with Della gone."

Carefully Kyle felt around with his foot, searching for a loose rock he could grab up and lob toward Locke. His boot scraped and Locke leapt toward Kyle, knife flashing. "Hey, don't you try nothin' funny here. We ain't got time to waste tonight. Winnie's going to need us and right soon, I fear. Let's head back to Oma's."

Then, to Kyle's astonishment, Locke reversed the knife in his hand. "Here. Hang on to it now. You're gonna need it."

Slowly, studying Locke's rough features, Kyle reached for the knife handle and tucked the weapon back into its sheath. Something in Locke's steady gaze puzzled him, casting doubt on his judgment of the burly farmer.

"We don't have to go back to Oma's," he said cautiously. "Wren should be turning up here fairly soon. In fact, I thought she might have reached here before me."

"How so?" Locke asked.

"She was coming by another route."

"There ain't no other way to here from Oma's."

Kyle's apprehension returned full force. "No? Porter said..."

"Porter?" Locke interrupted harshly. "She's with Porter, is she?"

Locke's sharp concern troubled Kyle and despite Porter's warning, he told him about the meeting at Oma's gate.

Locke listened tensely. "We've got to find them fast... afore it's too late. I wonder how much Wren knows or guesses? He may decide he has to kill her, even if she's...."

151

"Kill her?" echoed Kyle confusedly. "Why? Who?"

Locke's anxiety infected Kyle as the farmer plunged wildly back up the path toward Oma's. "Time's 'most gone," Locke muttered. "Where would he think to take her?"

Kyle grabbed for Locke's sleeve and missed his footing. He stumbled and swore at the tangled growth at his feet as well as at the mounting confusion in his mind. Wren was safe with Porter, wasn't she? Now Locke was behaving like her life was in danger from her own uncle. What the hell was going on?

Suddenly Locke checked in the road. "Did Porter tell you where the logging road was breaking through?"

"Yeh, he said it would be near here," Kyle frowned. "But we didn't see a thing torn up around here when we came in..."

"No, the scouts were marking trees further up...." Suddenly Locke's body tautened. "The Waitsel place! Where Della is buried! Must be where the Barrier is breached." Locke muttered. "Makes sense given all what's happened there."

Grabbing Kyle's arm, Locke crashed directly into the woods.

"Follow me as close as you can. Time's shortenin'."

Further up the mountain, Wren's breath came in ragged gasps as she and Porter struggled up a game trail zig-zagging over a rocky slope. Gradually she had realized that they were headed in the opposite direction of the Bentley place. Wren reluctantly admitted to herself there was something very strange about her uncle's behavior this night. He was mumbling to himself now but the rustling of leaves as a wind kicked up prevented Wren from distinguishing his words. He seemed to be carrying on a conversation with someone, a discussion both defensive and angry. Once Wren caught what sounded like her mother's name.

The blanket of fog began to unravel as the wind gusted

more strongly. Shadows leapt just beyond the edge of Wren's vision. Branches creaked and groaned overhead as Porter dragged Wren up a shale slope and across a bold creek that seemed familiar. The waters were tumbling around the stepping stones, talking to Wren as if they knew her. Suddenly, Wren recognized where she was... the ford through Lovada Branch she and Kyle had crossed with Mencie on the way to the Waitsel homeplace... and the site where Della's body lay under the rock cairn.

Had Porter known all along where his sister was buried? Wren's alarm heightened. Why had he never told Zettie? Had he guessed what Locke had done to Della and her horrible secret? If so, he might loathe Wren herself. What if....? Wren shrank from a thought that underscored her own sense of shame too clearly. She had no right to be alive. Her very existence might be what threatened the continuance of the community. If she were dead... would the Cove be safe?

Wren's mind lurched along with her feet. Did Zettie know? How could she not guess? Had she sent Wren out here this night with the intention or hope that she would be killed? Bitterness flooded Wren's heart and she faltered. Porter's lean hand snaked behind him and clamped her wrist. "Stay with me, girl," he hissed. "This night has been a long time coming." Then, sensing Wren's rising fears, he added gently, "You're safe with me, Winnie. I'm here to help you. You'll see."

"Of course," Wren thought gratefully. "Why else would he be trying to keep Locke away from me?" The very thought of Locke made her flesh crawl.

A storm was brewing and the trees about them bent and tossed as angry gusts lashed the forest. Wren heard a distant rumble and felt the ground shudder slightly underfoot. Thunder? Or something else? She'd seen no flash of lightning as yet.

153

Porter propelled Wren through a band of low shrubs into the clearing around the sagging Waitsel cabin. His breathing was harsh as they circled its dark bulk and headed for the stone cairn.

Some distance away, Kyle panted after Locke, fighting his way through tangled laurel breaks and tripping through treacherous witch hobble. Briar branches whipped against his face as he followed Locke's stocky form up a steep slope.

"Damn jungle," he swore, wiping blood and sweat off his face. Then he heard the rush of rock-strewn water and figured they were near one of the fords of Lovada Branch. Locke pushed on with a recklessness that spoke volumes to Kyle. They hardly noticed that the fog was being torn apart by gusts from the approaching storm. The ground trembled as thunder rumbled across the mountains.

Locke stopped so abruptly that Kyle stumbled into him.

"What was that?" Locke asked sharply.

"Thunder," growled Kyle.

"Not so sure." Locke sniffed the air and squinted. 'Din't see no lightnin' yet."

"Still on the other side of the mountain," Kyle responded impatiently. "Let's keep going."

"Hang on. Somethin's not right here."

"A lot isn't right!" Kyle retorted angrily, his anxiety to reach Wren nearly intolerable. He scanned the tossing trees and undergrowth impatiently. "Just a storm breaking. Move it, man."

Locke grunted and shook his head. "It's not far now. If we angle up this way, we'll hit the clearing just beyond the rock pile. With the woods so noisy, Porter may not hear us. We may even surprise him."

"What makes you so certain that we'll find him and Wren there?" Kyle asked as he unsheathed his knife and stepped warily back from Locke.

"Where else? *She's* here."

154

"She? You mean Della? How do you know she's buried there?"

"I helped Mencie that night," Locke responded heavily. "I didn't get there in time. Don't want that to happen again. We're going to have to move fast now," Locke added tersely. He studied Kyle, "Now don't you try to interfere with what you don't un'nerstand. 'Tain't really your affair."

"Anything that concerns Wren is my business," Kyle thought grimly as he followed Locke closely, clutching his knife.

In the clearing, Porter had flung Wren to the ground by the looming pile of rocks. Frightened by the crazed expression on his face, Wren clutched her shirt front, instinctively searching for the silver pendant. Her dismay mounted as Porter began furiously knocking out stones from the cairn beside her, muttering to himself.

"Don't have much time; have to get her away from here before...."

Wren leapt up and grabbed his arm. "Uncle Porter, what are you doing?"

"Out of my way, girl," he snarled, thrusting Wren back.

She staggered and would have fallen had not burly arms caught her up from behind. Startled, Wren twisted to find herself in Locke's grip. Her shriek strangled in her throat.

Abruptly, Locke thrust Wren toward Kyle and turned on his brother. "Porter, stop that! You can't hide this affair any longer. It's catching up with all of us now."

Porter clutched a rock in his hands and stared wildly at Locke. "What do you know about this, anyway?" he screamed above the roar of the trees.

"Most everything, brother," Locke said sadly and gently.

Shock crossed Porter's face. "How long?"

"Since we was boys."

"That long?" Porter squinted, "You never said anything...?" Locke shrugged but his hands twitched at his belt where a machete dangled.

Porter backed off, saliva glistening round his mouth. "You could've killed me ...."

Locke nodded and appraised Porter, contempt twisting his lips, "That wasn't for me to do, brother. God knows I wanted to, especially after I found Della here."

Porter shook his head, his eyes turning toward Wren. She stared back at him and then at Locke, comprehension slowly dawning.

"You?" she breathed. "*You* are my father?"

Porter said nothing as tears slowly formed and ran down his gaunt cheeks.

Wren groped, "You ... you're the one who raped Della?" Wordlessly, Porter lifted his hand and let it fall.

"You killed her, too?"

Porter's head jerked convulsively. "She died coming here too soon after you was born. Mencie told you the truth there. But yes, I'm as guilty of her death as ...."

"... you are of my birth!" Wren spat out.

Porter's long legs crumpled and he slipped to the ground, leaning against the cairn. His haunted eyes looked up at Wren. Locke and Kyle stepped back. Despite the growing tumult in the woods, Wren felt herself enclosed in a silent, private world with this man who had fathered her on his own sister. Porter slumped against the rocks entombing Della. Despite her loathing, Wren stepped slowly toward him, sinking down onto the grass until her face was on a level with Porter's.

"How could you have done such a thing?" she croaked. Porter shook his head, thin sandy hair falling over his forehead. "She was so pretty as a little girl. I ... we used to play a lot of 'love games' while Maw was at school, teaching. We stopped, of course, when Della grew older but that didn't change my wanting her in all the wrong ways. She sensed it-that's why she went off to work in Black Mountain as soon as she was old enough for hire. Maw never knew why she left ....," Porter's head dropped further.

"One Christmas when she came back, we were out in the 'bacca barn, just the two of us. Her hair was such a rich, pretty color - copper lights in it ... like yours, Winnie. I just ...just wanted to brush my hands through it. But she got angry, tried to push me away. I laughed when I realized she wasn't strong enough. And she pushing and pummeling me ... got me riled up like I'd never been before. I got her down and ... well, after I was done, she was crying and sobbing. Didn't say a word though. Didn't even look at me... just picked herself up and walked out of there... left Viney Branch that same day."

Spasms shook Wren as she fought off a gagging nausea. Her fingers scraped the grassy earth. Drawing in a deep breath, she forced herself to look at Porter. He was ashen; regret and guilt etched deep lines in a face suddenly shrunken and old. Wren struggled to hold onto the anger and hatred that had been her energy for years but despite herself, she felt them seeping away, leaving only a dead emptiness in their place.

Silently Kyle crept beside Wren, uncertain of Porter's next move. Wren gave no sign she heard him so he reached out to touch her elbow. She jumped as if shaking off a trance and before Kyle realized it, snatched the knife from his hand. When he made to grab it back, Wren shouldered him roughly aside.

She turned toward Porter, quivering with rage, the knife glimmering faintly. "You!" she began, her lips curling back over her teeth. The roaring in her ears merged with the thrashing of the rising storm. Lifelong grief and pain melded into pure fury, deafening Wren to all sounds but her own harsh sob.

But at that moment, Zettie's voice cut through the tumult in her mind. "Can you forgive?"

157

Wren shook her head violently."Why would I ever... ever do that? How could I?" Her breath came in short, angry gasps.

"You aren't able but the Spirit is." Zettie's soft voice continued. "What's the gain in keeping up this violence? It'll destroy you!"

"I was spawned of violence," Wren whispered.

Sweating despite the night's chill, Wren curved her fingers around the knife and stared directly into Porter's guilt-haunted eyes. Her vision blurred and she seemed to see a figure emerge from the stone cairn and kneel in the grass not far from Porter. The slim figure wore not the cold features of the mother she had imagined and hated since her teens but the frightened face of a young woman pregnant by incest and faced with dilemmas of life and death. "She chose life for me," Wren muttered, "though I should have never existed."

''These two are your blood's spring," a voice whispered in Wren's heart. Her eyes roved from the shimmer that marked Della's presence to the ghastly guilt-ridden face of Porter. Had Della forgiven him? Or did this unfinished task also rest with Wren?

Wren desperately wanted to flee but she somehow understood that the test she now faced would determine not only her future but the fate of The Cove as well. She clung to the memory of Zettie's words as a riptide of revulsion threatened to suck her beneath waves of hatred and despair. This man who had begotten her in selfish passion: this woman who had abandoned her... what claim had they on her compassion or forgiveness?

Kill him? Forgive him? Them? For what felt like an eternity, Wren clutched the knife, paralyzed, torn by passions and powers larger than her own personal horror, passions and powers that warred throughout the cosmos.

Beneath the roar of the approaching storm, Wren could hear (with curious clarity) the burbling of Lovada Branch as its waters swelled from rain in the uplands. With it, mingled many voices murmuring, "Mercy, mercy. Lord, have mercy!" Suddenly Wren recalled the other Cove members that Zettie and Jonah had sent out ahead of her. Were they near now, watching, waiting? Were they helping? Wren heard her own voice in the chorus, as well as those of Porter and Della, begging for the one thing they all desperately needed.

"O Lord, have mercy on us sinners," she sobbed, unaware she spoke aloud, startling the three men waiting warily in the clearing around her.

Very slowly Wren laid the knife on the breast of the earth. This land, too, had been ravaged and forced to bear unnatural fruits. Lightning flashed, briefly illuminating the clearing. Wren barely heard the crash of thunder that accompanied it as her soul reeled with a blinding vision - that of the mountain itself awaiting her choice, a choice that could either subject it to further destruction or liberate it to flourish renewed.

At this moment, it hinged on her. The decision was hers and hers alone. More than her own life and future 'hung fire' as Wren wrestled with her anger and loathing; the sense of filth that had infiltrated her whole being. Was there a Power great enough to overcome this sin? Wren now sensed Cove members praying in the darkness all around her.

Once more, her fingers closed around the knife and she smiled grimly. How good it would feel to wield it, to slash at this man who had violated his own sister, her mother. Wren struggled to her feet and stared down at Porter's contorted features, at his hapless drool. "I despise you!" she hissed.

Porter threw his head back, exposing his scrawny neck to her knife as if willing her to do for him what he had never had the courage to do for himself. For a long moment, Wren stared into the tortured eyes of the man who was her father. Raggedly she whispered, "Not for your sake but for mine

159

and hers; for something larger than any of us, I give you what is required."

She moistened her lips. "I forgive you. I can't hate anymore. No matter what I am, what you've made me, I don't have to be the channel of destruction you have been. I can't do to you what you did to her." She nodded toward Della's shade, hovering at the edge of the cairn. The soft shadow flowed toward Wren. Gentle hands wiped Wren's face as if thanking her for completing a task she had died trying to accomplish.

Porter stared at Wren with disbelief. "You... you forgive me?" he stuttered.

A heartbeat later, Wren added, "And Della forgives you, too, Porter. She wants you to know that."

Porter's bent frame heaved with racking sobs. Locke stepped over to his brother. Sensing his presence, Porter looked up. "Kill me," he pleaded, "I have no right to live."

Grimly Locke shook his head. "You're right, brother. But even to avenge my sister, I can't do it. If Winnie and Della forgive you, so must I."

Porter now turned hopefully to Kyle who had picked up his knife. "Will you ...?"

"End your misery, Porter?" The wind had dropped and an eerie silence filled the clearing. Kyle's jaw twitched, betraying a conflict raging within.He balanced the knife on his palm, as if looking at it for the answer. "No," he said finally and sheathed the knife.

Thunder rumbled again and the clearing shuddered. Trees crashed in the distance. Porter jumped and seemed to suddenly emerge from a trance. His teeth gleamed in a crazy grin. Suddenly he was laughing in loud raucous bursts.

Kyle yanked Wren away from this man whose hysteria frightened him even more than Porter's earlier desperation.

"No need to do anything now," Porter chortled. "It's too

late. They're almost here! The charges are going off!"

"Man, what are you talking about?" Locke shouted, reaching out to shake his brother. Porter dodged his hands and crawled swiftly behind the cairn still chuckling softly. "That's dynamite you're hearing, brother. The Service mined this whole area yesterday. The lightning must've set off the first of the charges ... they're on a successive timer...."

Locke swirled around as Kyle grabbed Wren roughly and tried to drag her out of the clearing. When Locke plunged after them, Wren dug in her heels. "We can't just leave him," she gasped.

"What the ....," Kyle began as Wren broke from his grasp and ran back toward Porter. She began tugging at his shirt. Locke and Kyle exchanged glances and then, hurrying back, reached down to drag Porter to his feet between them.

"Which way, brother, which way?" Locke demanded.

Porter only shook his head, demented laughter still bubbling from his throat.

Locke grunted in disgust. Kyle barked, "At least, let's get clear of this place!" and grabbing Wren he pulled her past the cabin and back under the trees. As in a nightmare the three men and Wren stumbled through the dark, storm-troubled forest fleeing a menace that could erupt under their feet at any moment. Suddenly, breaking free from Locke, Porter grabbed Wren and dashed towards a deep gully Lovada Branch had cut through the shale. At its rim, he paused, then roughly pushed her over the edge. Wren pitched forward, crying out as she fell. Kyle leapt after her. Locke turned on Porter but the taller man was running crookedly away from him, back toward the clearing.

A tremendous explosion rocked the mountain where the Waitsel cabin stood, the blast illuminating the figure of Porter dashing through the woods crying out Della's name. A rockslide thundering down the slope engulfed

Porter with a roar. Kyle felt Locke throw himself over the edge of the gully, forcing all of them deeper into the protection of the rocky banks of the branch.

A cloud of dust whistled over them, spattering small rocks and branches on their heads. As if in collusion, the sky opened and rain poured down, cleansing the gritty air and bathing the shuddering earth.

CHAPTER FIFTEEN

Huddling together under an outcropping of shale, Kyle, Wren and Locke waited until the torrent of rain had diminished to a soft drizzle. The rising waters of Lovada Branch finally forced them up and over the lip of the gully. There, in the lucent dawn, they beheld the devastation visited on the mountain during the night. Red earth, clotted with rocks and torn trees, bled down the slope before them. The rockslide had missed the gully by only a few yards.

Shaken and wordless, they surveyed the wounded mountain still moaning as the shredded forest shifted and settled in the sticky mud. Although Locke had a gash on his head and Wren's palms were scraped, none of the three had sustained any serious injuries. The flying debris had passed over their heads as they pressed up against the steep banks of the branch. The gully had proven the only refuge in the area although now the rising waters roiled with large branches and rocks that were gouging its walls and reshaping its bed.

"Is he....? Can we find him?" Wren ventured. The two men shook their heads helplessly. Porter seemed as gone as the stone cairn that had marked Della's lonely grave, both of them buried in the rubble uneasily settling around them.

Carefully, they began picking their way across the

blasted slope. Something glinting in the dim light caught Locke's eye. Reaching down he grabbed up a metal object and held it out to Wren.

"Recognize this?"

"My pendant!" she exclaimed, rubbing off the mud against her jeans. "How strange that it should be just lying there on top of all this...." Wren waved her arm about her. "It's as if I can't lose it."

Locke nodded slowly. "I've heard that's the case."

"What happened to your medal, Wren?" Kyle asked, "Did you drop it? The chain's gone."

'The chain broke when we left Oma's," Wren mumbled. "Porter noticed it and asked to "borrow" it. I was so confused that I didn't argue much once he said he needed it more than I. He talked about a rendezvous with its former owner, that it wouldn't help me anymore." Wren shuddered.

Locke frowned as Kyle asked, "What could he have meant by that?"

"Not sure," Locke muttered. "Did he plan to give it back to Della? What would have been the point in that? If'n he had, more than a chain would be broken... it'd break a whole line of...." His musing was interrupted when he caught sight of a gray shape flitting across the rockslide. It moved with the swift agility of a cat, leaping lightly from rock to rock. Waving her floppy gray hat, Mencie emerged through the groaning landscape. She sighed when she reached them, her wizened features appearing infinitely old and careworn in the pale light.

"You'ns all right?" she asked anxiously.

"We survived," Locke allowed dourly. "What about the rest of em?"

"None bad hurt," Mencie said, her eyes traveling swiftly over their muddied clothing. "Zettie's worried, of course." Mencie paused and looked around. "Porter?"

Wren's breath caught in her throat as Locke shook his head sadly. "Last we saw of him he was lopin' back toward the Waitsel place ... that was just back of when everthin' started slidin' down. Don't think anyone could've survived over there."

"So how come you did?" Mencie asked.

"Jest meant to, I guess," Locke responded with a shrug.

Wren broke in. "Porter grabbed me and threw me into the gully of the Branch."

"It looked to me like he was trying to kill Wren, throwing her down where she'd be either buried or drowned," Kyle added. "I jumped in after her and was about to pull her out when Locke landed on me, knocking the wind out of me."

"Twern't none of my doin'." Locke defended himself. "Porter dodged around me and gave me a shove from behind afore he took off into the woods again."

"What was he trying to do?" Wren asked. "Kill us or save us?"

For a moment, no one said anything. "No knowin', I guess," Locke finally admitted.

Decisively, Mencie beat her hat against her poncho, knocking off some encrusted mud. "Welp, the Barriers are closed again. The Cove is secure," she announced matter-of-factly.

"How can you say that?" Kyle exclaimed. "Look at this!" and he gestured toward the scarred mountainside.

"Mountain's heal, given time," Mencie replied. "Seems the Forest Service miscalculated what their charges would do in this area. The loggin' road they started has been completely blocked by this here rockslide."

"Will they give up then?"

"Only for a time," Mencie admitted. "But they can't come near The Cove now. The protections are secure again."

165

"Protections? What IS all this about barriers and gates and ... and protections?" Kyle pleaded in exasperation.

Mencie looked at Kyle as if he were particularly dense. "Fer a preacher and a shaman...," she shook her head mournfully. "The Cove is, as you should know, Kyle Makepeace, under God's Hand. But we have to be faithful to each other for that Protection to be effective. If each of us does our work and carries others' burdens as our own, the network of mercy prevails over and around us.

"Every so often that web gets strained and frays, as it were. It is up to the Guardians to be on the outlook fer this and call us to give account for our care of one another."

Kyle, stung by Mencie's rebuke shot back. "So tell me. What is *your* charge here in Lovada Cove?"

A thin smile flickered across Mencie's face. "I am the Warder in the Borderlands," she said softly. "I scan everyone who comes through here. Some I lead on in. Others? Well, they jest seem to end up walkin' round in circles and eventually find their way back out. A few, like Della ... and Porter now, get trapped here." She resettled her floppy hat over her braids.

For a few minutes no one spoke. "What frays the web of Protection over The Cove is betrayal by someone from The Cove itself," Mencie continued. "Winnie has closed the Gate for now. She's done the needful thing ... fer thet we're thankful."

Wren blushed at this unexpected tribute and awkwardly passed the back of her hand across her mouth, pressing back the tears evoked by the gratitude of Mencie, ageless doyen of the mountains.

"She's passed the first trial," Mencie admitted, 'but... as a Lovada woman she must complete her testing."

Wren stroked the silver disk still clasped in her hand. "Why did Porter want this?" she asked, hoping to divert Mencie from a subject she instinctively mistrusted. "How come I got it back? What am I to do with it?"

Mencie's sharp golden eyes probed Wren. "What Porter planned or thought, we'll never know. I doubt he understood what power lies with the woman to whom that pendant rightly belongs. Locke here, though, he can tell you," she responded cryptically.

Locke shot a dark look at Mencie before turning to Wren. "Maw, your Mamaw Winnie, and others were Keepers of the Spring in their time and then the charge passed to Della," he began slowly, "but Della wasn't able to complete her task. All she managed was to send you the token that would show you the way."

Locke indicated the disk Wren cradled in her palm. "She gave that to me just before she died and told me where to find you."

"Then you've known all along where I was! You were the stranger who gave this to my foster-mother for me," Wren gasped.

Locke nodded.

"Why didn't you tell Zettie?"

Locke gestured helplessly, "Della forbade me. She feared what Porter might do if he knew where you were, and like-as-not he would have found out, for Maw would have gone after you. I promised Della I would not betray her secret. She said you would find your own way here when the time came."

Wren studied the disk, so familiar and yet so strange. It grew warm in her palm and the faint etchings appeared more defined: the rippling water on the one side, the coiled snake on the other. It both attracted and repelled her.

"Even Mencie here doesn't know how to find The Spring," Locke continued, "though she sometimes goes along with a Keeper. Most everyone from The Cove has been to the Spring at least once. After that, it's just enough to know it's there." Locke was silent for a moment, nostalgia softening his weathered features.

Mencie's eyes brooded over Wren. "You must go to The Spring, Winnie Lovada, and learn what is required of you."

Wren continued to caress the shining disk, feeling it the only beautiful and untainted thing she could claim. "Am I to go alone?" she asked.

Amusement glinted in Mencie's deep eyes. "That's not for you to choose, girl. Only you as a Keeper can find the Spring or guide someone else there and back. But others may also need to find healing there," Mencie added mysteriously, her eyes flickering over Kyle.

Kyle frowned but before he or Wren could ask more, Mencie swirled her poncho around and walked away, disappearing quickly in the mist. Looking up, Kyle saw that the sky was growing brighter as the clouds of the past night dispersed.

Locke nodded to Wren. "I have something to tend to," he muttered, and struck out down the mountain.

Wren watched Kyle follow Locke with his eyes. "Don't you think you should go along with him?"

Kyle heard the rejection implicit in Wren's question and winced. "No, I believe we have something to 'tend to' also," he said quietly, reaching out to touch Wren's arm. But when she shrank back, Kyle dropped his hand helplessly. "Wren, let me help you. I love you, you know," he said softly.

"How can you? How can anyone love what I am?" Wren cried in anguish and jerked around to contemplate the raped mountainside surrounding them.

Wren's cry reminded Kyle of Belva's despairing whimpers as she plucked at her dead twins. "What can relieve such grief?" he pondered silently but no answer came to him.

Wren's bowed head and limp hands distressed Kyle. Even her hair seemed to have lost its customary bounce and vitality. Her mud streaked face looked drawn and lined in the harsh morning light. Even though Kyle now knew the full story of Wren's conception, the extent this knowledge had devastated Wren was beyond his comprehension. Never before had Wren shut him out like this and it was like a knife twisting in his heart, a grief sharper than what he had experienced at the death of his twin.

Somberly Kyle addressed his wife's slender back, "We must go to Zettie and tell her about Porter, Wren."

She shuddered and clutched the pendant more tightly but after a few moments of silent struggle, Wren slipped it into her breast pocket and turned, with a sigh of defeat, to face Kyle. "Who but me," she said despairingly. "If Locke couldn't tell her all these long years, I doubt he can do so now." Her eyes ranged over the ravaged landscape seeking some familiar landmark to guide them back to The Cove.

"If we follow the Branch, it will lead us back," Kyle offered and at Wren's nod, he set out ahead of her. Wren hesitated, her gaze sweeping over the muddy gash that now buried her parents. "Help me," she prayed as she turned to follow Kyle.

CHAPTER SIXTEEN

The midmorning sun shone hot on their shoulders when Wren and Kyle emerged from the shadows of the woods into the pastureland of The Cove. Across the fields, Zettie's little cabin looked forlorn with no chirpy little figure rocking on the porch. Anxiety hastened their steps until, as they drew closer, odors of bacon and biscuits and coffee assailed them. Then it was hunger that sent them flying up the steps and through the door into Zettie's welcoming kitchen.

Zettie's cheeks were flushed as she turned from the stove to greet them, her eyes searching and gentle. Kyle realized this tiny, white-haired woman already guessed everything so he said nothing, only put his arms around her silently. Zettie accepted his embrace gratefully and then reached out for Wren who hovered uncertainly behind Kyle.

"Come, dear," Zettie called softly and Wren allowed herself to be pressed up against the warmth of her Mamaw, who brushed her tangled hair back from her brow in a gesture that was both maternal and priestly. Wren dropped her head and let sobs shake her while Zettie held her crooning wordlessly, her tears mingling with Wren's.

"You did well, Winnie. I'm so proud of you," she said softly as Wren wiped her eyes on a handkerchief Zettie offered her.

"Mamaw," Wren began. "Mamaw, Porter's dead. He was killed in the rockslide from the dynamite blast."

"Yes, honey, I know."

"How? Did Locke tell you?"

"I was there, Winnie. When you called out for me, I heard you."

"Then, then you know about Porter and... and Della, about what happened?"

Zettie sighed regretfully. "Yes, I know... and have known far longer than I want to admit. I just couldn't face it although the truth was there for me to see if I'd had more courage. I hope you can forgive me, Winnie, as you forgave Porter."

"Oh, Mamaw!" Wren stepped back. "What is there to forgive?"

"I loved too blindly, Winnie," Zettie responded softly. "Come now and set yourselves down. Breakfast is ready." She turned from Wren back to her stove. Bearing platter and bowl, Zettie approached the table softly humming the chant they had first heard when following Mencie through the woods to Bewley and Haidia's, a variation on the old hymn "Were you there?" But the words that Wren caught now sounded like "Are you here at his rising from the dead?"

Gratefully, Wren and Kyle eased their tired bodies onto the chairs and allowed Zettie to place a bountiful breakfast before them. "Communion?" Kyle pondered briefly. They ate in silence, too exhausted for conversation that, they realized, wasn't necessary in the empathetic peace of Zettie's kitchen. Wren's eyes were drooping when her Mamaw led them to the bed they had hastily abandoned two nights previously. Kicking off their boots, they tumbled onto the pillows and fell into a deep, dreamless sleep.

Some hours later, Kyle stirred and sat up, puzzled briefly as to where he was. He must have fallen asleep before hitting the sheets. Beside him, Wren lay curled round herself, her breathing deep and even. The degree of

171

serenity that smoothed her features reassured Kyle. Only then did he focus on what had awakened him - a rhythmic rocking from the front porch where a burly figure occupied one of Zettie's chairs. The pungent aroma of pipe smoke drifted through the open window.

Slipping carefully out of bed, Kyle was surprised to realize he had been expecting Jonah. Boots in hand, he tip-toed out of the room and onto the porch, easing the door shut behind him. Crossing the weathered boards on bare feet, Kyle lowered himself to the steps where he stared off into the distance, absently massaging the scar on his foot.

Jonah drew deeply on the pipe clenched between his teeth and finally looked down to meet Kyle's questioning gaze. The hint of mirth in Jonah's appraising look irritated Kyle.

Brows knotted with suspicion of more unwelcome news, Kyle tugged viciously at the tangled laces of his boots.

With careful deliberation, Jonah knocked the dottle out of his pipe and drawled, "Son, first the socks. Then the boots."

Regarding the older man blankly for a moment, Kyle then studied his boots, discovering that his socks were stuffed into the toes. A reluctant grin tugged at the corners of his mouth as he glanced back at Jonah, "You still know how to reach me, don't you?"

Jonah continued to rock. "But reaching you and reading you are not the same thing."

"Meaning?"

"Tell me what's happening with you."

"What isn't happening?" Kyle snorted. "It's all so snarled up." He yanked irritably at the twisted bootlaces. "I have no idea where to start."

With patience born of years of listening, Jonah repeated, "Kyle, first the socks. Then the boots."

Kyle looking down, bit his lip, and drew a deep breath. "So,

172

okay, the socks. Jonah! Do you remember what it was like for you in the belly of the whale?"

Jonah nodded, eyes misting over. He rocked silently for a few minutes, the silence underlined by the droning of insects in the warm May sunlight and Kyle's efforts to retrieve the socks jammed into his boots.

Jonah waited.

"I don't know if she still loves me anymore," Kyle muttered at last, "I can't reach her. I don't know how to help her. She seems so far away from me now."

"She is," Jonah said softly, adding "Maybe you can't help her."

Kyle looked up in anguish, "But I'm supposed to be a healer!"

Jonah looked steadily, questioningly, at the younger man.

"Am I not?"

"Depends."

"On what?"

"He who does not gather with me, scatters," Jonah said cryptically.

Kyle flinched.

"Face it, Kyle. Ugly as that scar is," Jonah said pointing to Kyle's heel, "it's not near as ugly as the vengeance you swore against The Healer when you were ordained. You set yourself on a path that is destroying you and just now damn near destroyed us! You've twisted and turned inside out a power that was meant for good and you have the nerve to ask now, 'Why can't I heal?'!"

Kyle dropped his head into his hands; his shoulders slumped. As sweat ran down his armpits, Kyle could feel defiance oozing out of him to be replaced by fear. Truth! Astringent as a dose of bitter herbs! Finally, shaking his head, he asked in a strangled voice, "So what can I do?"

"Do?"

"Should I leave?"

"Again? Hell, no! You think you can keep on running from the Living God?"

"Then what, Jonah?"

The hardness in Jonah's eyes softened and the same gentle mirth returned. He shifted in his chair and leaned towards Kyle. Almost in a whisper, he said, "Say 'uncle.'"

"Say what?"

"Say 'uncle.' He's beaten you, hasn't he? If I am Jonah, Kyle, you are Jacob."

Staring off across the pastureland to the mountains beyond,
Kyle absorbed Jonah's insight and nodded slowly to himself. He had spent his life wrestling with God but only now could he see how hopeless a task it was. Still....

"If I am Jacob, I'm not letting go until He blesses me," Kyle quoted stubbornly.

"So He will, son," Jonah ruminated, "so He will." Carefully, Jonah refilled his pipe and puffed on it until it was drawing satisfactorily. "Just be sure you recognize the blessing when it comes."

Again, Kyle flinched.

Wren wakened a half-hour later to the rhythm of a rocker punctuated by the crunch of gravel as Kyle paced back and forth on the road, limping slightly, as if the scar on his foot pained him.

The fragrance of freshly baked bread teased Wren out of bed and into the kitchen where Zettie sat shucking a pan of early peas. Tugging at her rumpled clothing, Wren's hand brushed across the silver pendant and she drew it out from her pocket.

"Mamaw," she began, and Zettie nodded her toward a chair drawn up across from her. Her hands slowed and she smiled up at Wren encouragingly.

"Do you know what this is?" Wren asked holding out the shiny disk. "Have you seen this before?"

Zettie took it into her work-worn hands carefully and as she studied it, a mystified expression crossed her face. When Wren stirred, Zettie looked up, puzzled.

"Yes, I've seen this before. I gave it to your mother when she became a young woman ... just as my Maw would have given one like it to me had she not died so early. Mencie kept mine for me until I was ready."

"Ready?"

"To take on the responsibilities of a Lovada woman; to accept my charge as Keeper of the Spring."

Wren wrinkled her brow. "Mencie used that phrase this morning but she wouldn't tell me what it meant. It was Locke who told me you were a Keeper once."

Zettie thoughtfully laid the pendant on a napkin. To the younger woman it seemed to glow with new luster. "Do you know why your middle name is Lovada, Winnie?"

"Isn't it a hereditary thing in our family," Wren said, "that a girl child of each generation carry that name?"

"Something like that. The one who is a Keeper of the Spring is more a guardian of the life-spirit of the people than a Healer or Leader. Our role is to keep the people connected to their source. We don't let folks forget where to find the living water. Sometimes we give it to them; sometimes we show them where to find it for themselves."

"I can't do that!" Wren cried out in agitation. "It requires someone holy and... and clean. Not a, a thing like me." Abruptly she seized the disk to hurl it away from her but Zettie grabbed Wren's wrist firmly.

"Winnie Lovada," she said roughly. "You have carried this token almost since birth. Whether you want it or not, the task is yours. As Mencie told you, you must go to the Spring and find out what is required of you."

Just then the front door slammed and they heard Kyle's boots accompanied by Jonah's heavier footfalls.

"And furthermore, you will take Kyle with you," Zettie

added in a voice that brooked no argument.

As the men entered the kitchen, Zettie jumped up announcing brightly, "Supper's comin' on ready. Oma and Anson Jack are stoppin' by. Jonah, you and Kyle get the extra boards for the table from the shed. Winnie, finish up these peas while I see to the ham."

By the time Oma and Anson Jack arrived, the long table was spread with a clean cloth and six places set. Oma's contribution of her justly famous sweet potato pie steamed at one end. Anson's homemade Muscadine wine gleamed in a large pewter cup. Wren set the ham on the table near Jonah's place and turned to retrieve a bowl of peas from the warming oven. Zettie placed a loaf of new bread in a basket at the center of the table and positioned the pewter cup at Kyle's place, together with a white napkin. Hearing his strangled gasp, Wren glanced over her shoulder.

"No!" Kyle whispered harshly, backing away from the table. Wren watched his struggle and wondered at her own indifference. His pain couldn't touch her for now she had no claim on Kyle - as a husband or a friend. She set the peas on the table, curious about what was developing but sadly aware of how distant it was from her.

Under the intense scrutiny of the white-bearded man across the table, dismay welled up in Kyle.

"I can't! No one knows better than you that I shouldn't ....," he began.

"Yes, son, we know," the older man responded in a deep voice. "But we don't take account of worthiness around here. Nor does God. Jacob was the wiliest wheeler and dealer the Bible ever mentions. Did that stop God from blessing him or prevent him from offering acceptable gifts?"

Kyle narrowed his eyes, trying to assess Jonah's motivation. His hands gripped the chair back until his knuckles gleamed white. Voices from the past reminded him of his vow of revenge but also of repeated mercies. In the lengthening silence, the intensity of Kyle's struggle struck Wren like repeated blows. Zettie, Oma, and the others regarded him tenderly. Wren felt their prayers enwrap both of them as gently as a spring breeze teasing open a new leaf.

Kyle drew an unsteady breath and touched Wren's arm, mutely asking her help. Wren said nothing but did not pull away. Slowly she took her place at Kyle's side, hesitation clouding her blue-green eyes. She had no right to him now anyway - why hinder his reclaiming a priesthood, a rival with which she could never compete?

Zettie picked up the breadbasket, raised it in a silent gesture and then offered it to Kyle. He could not refuse to accept it from her gnarled hands and as he did so, insight bloomed. Zettie was offering him a share in *her* priesthood, a priesthood that she held as woman, as mother, as member of The Cove ... and also, Kyle realized, as member of the human race. Her priesthood devolved from roots far deeper than the one he held as an ordained minister.

By offering him the bread she had baked with her own hands, Zettie was tendering him an incomparable gift, one he could no more refuse than the gift bestowed by Belva. Kyle would have knelt as he accepted the bread but he suspected he might embarrass this motherly elder so he merely bowed his head to her, cupping his hands to receive the holy basket.

As he did so, he remembered the haunting scriptural image of Melchizedek who had met Abraham returning from battle with the kings and had blessed him. This mysterious figure, priest of a religion more ancient than the patriarchs, had offered bread and wine in a rite that embodied humanity's enduring need to worship. Kyle glanced at the elders gathered around Zettie's table, recognizing in them a long, long line of priestly people.

Elevating the basket, Kyle silently offered this acceptable gift to the Most High and, at the same time, begged for grace to be true to his own humanity. Oma and Anson Jack clasped hands; Jonah and Zettie beamed at him from either end of the table. Only Wren seemed unable to understand this communal offering.

Hesitantly Kyle reached for the pewter cup. Cradling it in his sun-browned hands, he swirled the wine as if reading a message there.

"Father, forgive me," he murmured.

"Father, forgive us all," the circle of prayers echoed, and Kyle was pleased to hear Wren's voice softly joining them. She knew so much more about forgiveness than he, Kyle thought, remembering the tumultuous night just past. This wine represented her gift more than his and Kyle wanted to hand the Cup to her to offer. But her closed face and distant look prevented him from following this impulse. Instead he mentally mingled her pain and his in the golden wine and whispered: "May the Maker of all life bless this food and drink as body and blood shared unto Salvation."

"Amen!" responded those gathered in Zettie's kitchen. "Amen!" echoed the Cove surrounding them.

The bread and wine were handed round. When they reached Wren, she hesitated but to Kyle's relief, did not refuse them. An evening chorus of birds in the surrounding woods filled the kitchen as bowls and platters were emptied amid the peaceful conversation that Jonah sparked. When Wren dared look into the faces about her, they mirrored a serenity she envied but could not herself share. These were whole people, rightly made, worthy to have a place in the world. But she....

The disk, restrung and resting again between her breasts grew so warm it felt like fire against her skin. Wren reached for it and a tiny flicker of hope leapt through her unbidden. Tomorrow she would go to the Spring.

CHAPTER SEVENTEEN

"Go, Keeper of the Spring, you have a journey ahead of you," Zettie murmured to Wren the next morning as Kyle and she stepped off Zettie's front porch onto the dewy grass. Dawn-light glowed behind the peaks surrounding The Cove but shades of night still lingered under the trees.

Wren merely nodded, her mouth set in a straight line and turned purposefully toward Lovada Branch, tumbling down the mountainside. A rough path ran along it, edged with wild strawberries and bright buttercups. For some hours, Kyle followed Wren as the trail snaked upwards through the woods until the trees thinned out and the slope grew rockier. They hiked silently, absorbed in private battles that blocked their once free and easy companionship.

Lovada Branch continued to narrow until it was a mere shimmer of light sliding soundlessly over smooth stones. Without warning it disappeared under a boulder the size of a house, bringing Wren and Kyle to a halt. They stood at the edge of a bald, a high natural grassland devoid of trees.

"So now?" Kyle asked, arching his eyebrows at Wren.

Wren smiled grimly. "I hope the mountain won't savage us... as it has others." She began to wander around the boulder with deep concentration, touching the silver disk

179

that now glimmered outside her shirt. When she reached the far side of the boulder, she looked up suddenly. "It's here, Kyle. I can feel water flowing deep below. My feet and legs are tingling."

Kyle stood beside her and shook his head. "I don't feel a thing," he admitted.

"No, you wouldn't," Wren replied absently as she began to pace slowly, straining to sense where the water flowed beneath the surface. Clutching the pendent, Wren gradually picked her way with increasing certitude. Kyle followed, expecting they would continue to climb but Wren was taking a slightly downhill course that veered eastward. They entered a copse of trees, unusually lush at this elevation, and Kyle wondered if their roots were tapping into the underground stream.

The rough rock over which they had walked gave way to grasses studded with wildflowers. They slipped out of the sun into the shadow of a weathered granite cliff sparkling with mica. Wren touched the rock reverently. "How old this is!" she murmured to herself. Far beneath her feet, she could feel water rushing with surprising force. Her whole body tingled now and she felt pressure on her ears. Penetrating deeper into this shaded gorge where rock walls rose on both sides of them, Wren realized the "pressure" was the roar of a not-too-distant waterfall.

Eagerly Wren began to trot and Kyle stretched his legs to keep up with her. The gorge narrowed until the shrubby laurel clinging to the rocks entwined overhead. "A dead end." Kyle thought and was about to suggest they turn back when Wren disappeared from his sight.

In the gloom of the ravine, Wren had caught a glimmer of sunlight among the fronds of a small hemlock. Crawling beneath its branches, she had discovered a narrow cleft in the rock wall behind it. She was about to slide through but an invisible force halted her. Kyle was not with her.

180

Beyond the cleft. Wren could see sunlight playing over shiny laurel leaves still decked with blossoms. The waterfall sounded closer, its roar mingling with the splashing of a rocky brook.

Again she tried to pass through but the barrier held. Impatiently, Wren twisted around and crawled back to the whispering evergreen.

To Kyle, puzzled and worried, Wren seemed to spring like a wood sprite out of the hemlock itself. Her face was impatient as she brusquely gestured him to follow her. Kyle was reminded of a child who had discovered a secret hiding place she was reluctant to share. He dropped to his knees to follow Wren's crouching figure.

Only then did Kyle see the fissure in the rock wall. The light pouring through it winked out as Wren slid through but then shone again. The passage was so narrow that Kyle had to slip off his knapsack and even the knife sheathed to his belt. Loathe to lose these supplies and protection, he tried dragging them behind him as he squeezed through. But the opening seemed narrower than before. Only after Kyle reluctantly tossed them back under the hemlock, did the fissure admit him.

He found Wren waiting for him as he emerged blinking, into the pouring sunlight. Fear and awe mingled in her eyes. In an unexpected (of late) gesture of intimacy, Wren reached for Kyle's hand as they walked into the Eden-like freshness of this hidden valley. The air caressed them, filled with woodland aromas and the trilling of numberless birds. Wren and Kyle bowed to the unseen Guardians of this holy place, petitioning pardon and grace to enter a sanctuary that seemed to predate time.

Goldfinches swooped in and out of the shadows of gigantic laurel while electric blue indigo buntings flashed about. Scarlet tanagers flitted among the tallest branches and the melody of a Baltimore oriole's courtship song

181

flowed over them. Kyle almost forgot to breathe, reveling in the sensual and spiritual *elan* that flooded through him. He suspected that Wren was leading him into a Garden of God, preserved among these most ancient mountains on earth.

Wren, her defenses momentarily breached, turned her face to the sun, arms spread wide in helpless wonder. Home! She was home at last where healing and cleansing....! Wren's heart crumpled. "No," she shook her head, "No, not for her."

Who was she to stand in this holy place? Suddenly alarmed, Wren ducked out of the sunlight into the shelter of the shrubs. Gentle laughter startled her. Did it come from the whispering trees? The chuckling brook? Wherever it came from, the lilting sound conveyed total affection; non-judgmental and freely offered. Sharp tears stung Wren's eyes and she drew in a shuddering breath. Dare she dream the impossible?

A shadow crossed her half-open eyes and Wren peered round a massive tree trunk to see Kyle looking about him apprehensively. He, too, had heard the soft laughter and was as mystified as she. Allied by their mutual forebodings and wonderment, they walked side by side deeper into the glen. The sunlight played over Kyle's full silvery hair and evoked fiery flickers from Wren's darker tresses. An invitation to dance teased their reluctant feet but dread dragged their heels. The sound of a rushing falls drew them on inexorably. Rounding a stand of Great Laurel still in full bloom, they halted, dumbstruck, on a mossy bank.

Involuntarily reaching again for each other's hands, Kyle and Wren slowly lifted their faces to what they knew was the glory of this sacred grotto. Thirty feet above them, spraying skyward in the clear morning light, the Spring leapt high and free of its rocky confines. Falling back like a fountain, it tumbled down amid foam and mist to a glassy

The *Spring*

green pool. Though narrow in span, the force of the falls shook the ground beneath them. Beholding it, caught up in this marriage of water and light, Wren's whole body responded in orgasmic delight. Even in her moments of most passionate love-making with Kyle she had never experienced such a transport.

The Spring, the true source of Lovada Branch, played and shimmered before their dazzled vision. Kyle squinted upward while Wren shaded her eyes with a trembling hand. Wave upon wave of wonder washed over and through her until Wren felt she could bear no more. She looked at Kyle who was drinking in the sight with the intensity of a shaman vouchsafed the fulfillment of his life's quest. How distant he seemed from her in this moment.

Kyle felt Wren's eyes upon him and leaned toward her, his face reflecting a joy she could not share. Slowly she backed away. For a moment, all her bitterness and pain had vanished. But now they rushed back, suffocating the brief hope the leaping spring had evoked.

Unable to bear more conflict, Wren fled behind the Great Laurel where she was shielded from the vision of a purity and grace that could never be hers. Leaning into the sheltering branches, she accidentally knocked off one of the pale blossoms and caught it as it fell. She was still twisting it wistfully in her hands when Kyle sat beside her.

"You are the Keeper of this wonder," he murmured reverently.

Wren shook her head slowly. She shouldn't be... in fact, she shouldn't exist at all. A honeybee buzzed past her ear and alighted on the flower in her hands, drinking eagerly of the sweet nectar. Wren held herself steady, humbly grateful that she could be of momentary service to one small marvel in a world too holy for her presence.

She shuddered. "I can never be worthy to be a Keeper of such a, such a ...," her voice trailed off.

Kyle touched her arm. "Does worthiness matter here, Wren? As Jonah reminded me, no one is worthy to share... or to minister the Mysteries." He paused, then mumbled mockingly, "Least of all me. Why was I chosen? How can I escape? Damned if I accept, damned if I don't!" He laughed mirthlessly.

Wren wrinkled her brow at Kyle. What was he talking about? He didn't carry the stigma she did. Did he? Kyle was rambling on about Mencie saying that more than just their own lives were at stake here. She didn't get it ... didn't want it. But Kyle began to confide to her his recent encounter with Belva and his confrontation with Mencie.

Wren listened in fear, bewilderment, and growing shock as Kyle's story unfolded. He was struggling to convey his frustration about reclaiming his Cherokee heritage, when she broke in roughly: "So, what more have you been hiding from me, Kyle Makepeace? You never told me you had a twin; the story you gave me about your scarred foot was a lie....," Wren was breathing heavily. "And you've been mocking the God to whom my people have entrusted their very lives!"

Kyle's shoulders sagged and he turned away from her fury, feeling it was more than justified. He had rejected the shaman-hood out of guilt and anger at the loss of his twin; he had seized ordination for purposes of defiance and vengeance. For all of this, he deserved to be the outcast he had long held himself to be. But Jonah and Mencie had both been adamant that this was the coward's way out ... that it was no longer an option for him to run from his destiny... or his God.

Kyle rubbed his hands in desperation and confessed to Wren, "I can't run any more. The old wounds are all open again and my energy... mostly anger, is gone. All I have left is regret... I'm drained... and just too tired to even care." The stony look Wren shot at Kyle bespoke no pity but rather, it seemed to him, loathing of his multiple betrayals.

But when Wren opened her mouth, no words came out- only a strangled cry of despair. What hope existed for either of them?

"Why not just kill me?" he asked bleakly. "If there is any such thing as a sin against the Holy Spirit, it has to be what I have done."

"No, there is worse," Wren reflected bitterly, as Kyle heaved himself to his feet and shambled off. Wren remained, hugging her knees in the cool shade and wondering if she believed her own words.

For a while, the valley's music soothed the inner clamor that had deafened Wren since she had learned of the incest. Then despair roiled through her again. She was the rotten spawn of an unspeakably ugly act and nothing could change that... facts were facts, weren't they? Wren rubbed her burning eyes.

Mencie's words came back to her. "As a Lovada woman you must complete your testing. At the Spring you will learn what is required of you."

Stoically Wren arose and returned to the falls again. The sun now shone more directly into the water, creating rainbows amid the leaping spray. Mesmerized, Wren drew closer and closer to where the white water foamed down into the swirling green pool at its base.

Despite her dread of its power, she began to step from rock to rock heading directly toward the plunging torrent. The roar deafened her and Wren was soaked when she reached the face of the falls. She thrust her hand into the falling water. It was slapped back at her so forcefully she almost lost her balance.

Peering through the shimmering screen, Wren perceived a dark area like a cave beyond the veil of mist and knew that was her goal. She carefully retraced her steps across the slippery rocks, intending to slip behind the waterfall from the side. But that proved impossible. The only way into the cave was through the thundering waters.

Wren briefly debated telling Kyle where she was going but decided against it. This was something she must do alone. She removed her boots and hobbled barefoot over the stepping stones piercing the turbulent waters, determined to plunge through the falls fully aware that the white water could pound her to death on these rocks. Drawing a deep breath, Wren lowered her head, closed her eyes, and leapt at the water, heedless of what would happen. Would she be rejected? Would she drown? The force of the white water knocked her down and under the surface. Blindly she felt a disorienting world of noise and wet engulf her. Suddenly the pressure let up and Wren bobbed up in the calmer water behind the falls, scraping her knees in rocky shallows.

Opening her eyes, she pushed back her dripping hair and crawled up the stony slope into a room-like cave. The roar was not so deafening within the confines of the grotto. Wren stumbled to her feet and recovered her breath. Light shimmered across the walls causing the mica imbedded in the stone to sparkle like crystal.

The continual movement dazzled Wren so that at first she did not notice the shadow rippling across the back of the cave. Something long and dark slithered down the wall. Wren froze. A black snake as thick as her leg slid soundlessly to the floor a yard from her bare feet.

Mindless fear assailing her, Wren poised for flight. But her body would not respond and she stared hypnotized at the sinuous black length writhing toward her. The snake's smooth skin slid across her left foot and she opened her mouth in a silent scream. Panic clutched Wren, all her serpent nightmares reviving in brilliant clarity. Perhaps this was just another dream? Perhaps she had fallen asleep under the laurel?

187

Wren flung out her arm and grimaced as her hand scraped against the all-too-real granite. Meanwhile the snake turned and flowed up onto a table-like formation in the center of the grotto where it coiled itself and regarded Wren with a steady, dark gaze. Sucking her bloodied knuckle, Wren stared back, drawing a long shuddering breath. Her foot was unscathed; she had been neither bitten nor bruised. Her worst fear realized, she yet lived.

Suddenly weak, Wren sat down on the hard floor. The snake did not move and Wren had the uncanny feeling that it was waiting for her to do something. She craved escape but dreaded the passage back through the falls. While she fought to control her hysteria, Wren's eyes darted about the shallow cave. It was an arched grotto about ten feet high entirely curtained by white water. The quartz rock where the black snake coiled reminded Wren of an altar.

Hypnotized by the unblinking stare of the snake, Wren felt herself sinking into a profound trance. Little by little, her body relaxed; her mind calming and focusing. As she gazed at the shimmering coils of the snake, Wren was struck by its seductive beauty. She could understand now how ancient cultures could regard this graceful creature as an emblem of healing and wisdom. Wren recognized her desperate need for both and a deep yearning welled up within her, a silent plea for health and wholeness.

With unshakable certainty, she knew that all the women who had been Keepers of the Spring before her had met this black snake behind the shimmering veil of the falls. Wren had come to the place and time of testing that Mencie had foretold. What would be asked, nay, required of her?

As if in answer to this question, a floating sensation lifted Wren and she felt, rather than heard, the rhythmic rush and flow of waters pulsing as if to her mother's heartbeat.

A voice, so familiar and so early in her memory it may have been imprinted on her in the womb, resounded through

Wren. A woman whispered, "Listen, child, listen. Oh, please, hear me and believe. I love you. Whatever has happened or will happen, I chose not to take your life. I don't know if you will be born normal; I don't know how I will be able to do for you ... or protect you from hurtful things..."

The strained voice broke, paused and then continued fiercely, "No! Nothing and no one shall hurt my little'un! However I've come by you, baby, I want to do right by you now. I'll take you home ... home to The Cove."

Wren felt a tender pressure, as if, while she still lay in the womb, her mother had wrapped her arms across her belly, determined to shield her unborn child from anything hateful or hurtful. "Take my child, Lord, take this little'un," Della pleaded. "Let no other claim her."

Bell-like, syllables from scripture rang through Wren's body until her whole being thrummed. *"You are Mine,"* says the Lord God.

"God's?" Wren whispered. Her first reaction, typically, was resentment. Why, if she were God's, had she been conceived under such monstrous circumstances? Slowly, like oil oozing into dried leather, softening and tenderizing it, the words formed a melody and rhythm that rocked and soothed her. "You are mine, you are mine...."

Tears streamed silently down Wren's cheeks, released (it seemed) from reservoirs dammed up from before her birth. Blinded by their salty sting, Wren rocked back and forth on the stony floor, losing all track of time, as every cell in her body tingled, surrendering to a love she did not have to deserve and which would never abandon her.

"WINNIE LOVADA, WHY ARE YOU HERE?"

Her trance suddenly shattered, Wren leapt to her feet and stared around. No one else was in the grotto, just herself and the black snake, motionless as carved ebony, on the altar-rock. The mica glittered around her and the roaring water created a room of silence that held Wren

189

captive. This Voice had not spoken from the past but boomed out of the Present. Why am I here? Because I am worthy? Wren blanched and her lips curled in familiar self-contempt. Hardly that! Then why? Because I am so needy? Yes! Desperately needy, heartbreakingly forlorn and needy!

"God, help me!" she anguished, pitching herself forward on her knees towards the altar-rock. Suddenly she saw her self-loathing for what it was, a product of her pride, not a fruit of self-acceptance. Her conception by incest made her like all those she had so easily dismissed as the losers, the useless and worthless members of society. Anger at all the circumstances of her life and hatred she dared not direct at God had been aimed at the most vulnerable person to hand, herself

She couldn't, shouldn't be like *them*. In the past, she had always imagined a division, a separation between herself and them, the shiftless, the needy, the... trash. Now she was one of them and she hated it, hated herself because she was no better than... well, all the rest. What arrogance to have thought she was better or, for that matter, worse than the rest of humanity? What, what stupidity! With a snort of derisive laughter, Wren's chin dropped to her chest.

How could she still be loved or wanted by anyone ... by Kyle? by God? Yet, in this hidden, holy place, under the steady gaze of the black snake, Wren knew in her bones that she was loved, accepted, cherished. The dark hole down which she had felt herself falling suddenly had a bottom; an ultimate place of security that would never fail her. She was securely held, no matter how hard or long she kicked against the Holder.

"Stop fighting, you silly ass," Wren whispered and a trace of a grin touched her lips. "Give up. Surrender, idiot!" Wren's shoulders sagged but this time it was because a great weight was being lifted off them, off her heart.

Acceptance of herself as she was, acceptance that allowed for no bartering; acceptance that included all the rest of her brothers and sisters...., nothing more, nothing less ... this was what was required of her.

"I am a child of incest, bastard born, abandoned ... and it doesn't matter," she mouthed, testing the words. The black snake rippled but remained coiled only a few inches from Wren's bowed head. She lifted her hands, laid them on the stone beside the ropy body of the snake where they gleamed slender, white, mutely pure. Wren whispered, "Lord, forgive me for rejecting what I am, for having rejected You and who You are. Even so, You have never left me, never ceased to call me your own!"

Nearly forgotten words gushed up from her memory: *"God chose those whom the world considers absurd to shame the wise; he singled out the weak of this world to shame the strong. He chose the world's lowborn and despised, those who count for nothing..."* Wren smiled wryly and nodded, "Ah yes, lowborn and despised ..." That she certainly was. What could such as she do for others? But even as she mocked herself, other words forced themselves into Wren's awareness:

"I have given you example. As I have done for you, so you also must do."

Wren's eyes flew open. "To accept everyone just as they are - to accept myself ... not to judge," she sighed deeply, "but to simply "do" for others ... with love. How could she do this in truth and not pure fantasy?

A picture of herself waiting on tables rose in Wren's mind. Elderly men and women were sitting in a warm dingy room. She recognized it as the dining room of the Senior Center in the village of Laurel Spring. In the past, Wren had pitied not only the people who went there but also those who staffed the place, suspecting they were folks unqualified for any better job. What was she doing among them?

Inexorably the vision unfolded and Wren saw herself kneeling, basin and towel in hand, begging to wash callused, yellow feet stuck into scuffed shoes and ragged slippers. Did they know who and what sort of woman was about to touch them? They did and their wise and gentle eyes welcomed her.

Both resistance and defenses fell away from Wren when, in her inner eye, she beheld old Gaither take the towel and basin from her and bid her be seated. Tucking the towel into his frayed red braces, he gently bathed her cold feet and rubbed them warm and dry between his gnarled hands.

As the shimmering water cascaded behind her, Wren wrestled with the vision and its implicit call to serve and be served in ways she had never considered. Despite the chill from her wet clothes, Wren felt perspiration on her upper lip. What was she being asked to do?

A scaly, scraping noise roused Wren and she quivered with shock. The sinewy black snake was gliding over her hands. In frozen dread, Wren felt the snake slither across her wrists and down behind the stone, disappearing into a hole in the granite floor. Wren's wrists and hands glistened in the wavering light of the grotto. She lifted them closer to her face, amazed to see oil, clear and rich, dripping from her fingertips. Wren raked her hands through her hair, smoothed them across her brow and down her tear-streaked cheeks. Like healing balm, the fragrant oil soothed and strengthened her.

Unbidden, the fact of Kyle's anointing and ordination intruded on her fragile calm, shattering it with grief and a sense of betrayal larger even than the anger she had borne toward her mother. No longer could she regard Kyle as her husband ... but hard as she tried to hate him, it was her love for this man who could never be... and never was? ... her husband that twisted knife-like in her bosom. His calling, whether he was true to it or not, left her with no future, a false past. Life stretched ahead of her empty and barren. Wren's groan of anguish was drowned by the powerful roar of the falls.

A flicker on the altar where the snake had been coiled caught Wren's attention. Peering closer, she discovered a small pile of tarnished silver coins. When she held one up to the light, however, she saw it was not a coin but a pendant pierced with a small hole. A rough but familiar design was still discernable despite mold and dirt, a series of rippled lines on one side; a spiral scratched on the other. Wren rubbed it hard between her fingers to confirm her suspicions. No doubt about it - it matched the etchings on the silver disk she wore beneath her tee shirt. Some of the "coins" looked very worn and thin; others less so. A few were dented and jagged as if they had seen rough usage.

The women who had preceded Wren to the Spring must have left these here. One of the pendants was scraped and bent out of shape. As soon as she picked it up, Wren realized it had been Zettie's. Holding it, Wren felt something of the anguish her Mamaw had carried for so many years. It was as if she held Zettie's worn old heart in her hands.

She was still staring at the disks when she heard a distant shout and recognized Kyle's voice. Her heart clenched painfully. Wren slipped the chain over her head and laid her own pendant on the altar beside the others, the disk that was both hers and Della's. She could not leave the sanctuary without offering sacrifice - as had the women before her.

Her hand still resting on the pendant, Wren seemed to hear a soft "Thank you, daughter." breathed into her ear. A task was completed, a link closed in an unbroken chain that stretched back as far as memory. Still Wren hesitated. Would she be able to find her way back to the Spring

193

without the disk? It was a risk she must take. If she were meant to return, she would find the way.

Wren grasped the edge of the stone altar about to drag herself up off her aching knees. A chinking sound arrested her. Her wedding ring had struck against the rocky edge. Sagging back on her heels, Wren contemplated the gold circlet through tear dimmed eyes. Grabbing her left hand, she tugged viciously at the ring until, with bruising pain, it slid over her knuckle and lay, glowing dully, in her right palm. Another thing to leave behind, she thought sadly. She flung it into the rushing water behind her before she could change her mind. Her marriage, or what she had thought was her marriage, was over.

CHAPTER EIGHTEEN

Once more Kyle's voice drifted through the roar of the falls. "Wren, Wren, where are you? Winnie Lovada, can you hear me?" His cry was sharp with anxiety.

Returning to the Great Laurel where he had left Wren, Kyle was distraught to find her gone. His apprehension was not relieved when he discovered her boots at the edge of the deep pool. Wren was not much of a swimmer and this turbulent water was treacherous even for the most experienced. Kyle paced along the rocky edge, reliving his own recent plunge into the waters of Lovada Branch.

After leaving Wren half-asleep under the Great Laurel, Kyle had stumbled blindly along the brook that bubbled through the valley. The merry sound resembled a chuckling mockery of his anger at a God who had tricked him into a wrestling match he could never win. Through clenched teeth Kyle growled, "I won't let go until You bless me!"

Without warning, Kyle found himself pitched into the rushing water of Lovada Branch and swept into a deep pool. Sputtering he breached the surface, only to crash his head against an overhanging rock and to sink again, stunned and disoriented.

Kyle felt his scarred heel scrape the bottom and instinctively thrust upward again. He burst out of the water,

195

gasped a mouthful of air and was tumbled into a whirlpool that bashed him against another boulder. He could find no hold on the slippery surface and felt himself being sucked back under the swirling froth.

Through gritted teeth, Kyle grunted, "I asked to be blessed, not drowned, You!" Once again the water chuckled and as it did so, Kyle found himself tossed into a quiet eddy behind a rock. Gasping, he threw himself onto the grassy bank, bruised from head to foot.

"*WHAT IS YOUR NAME?*" echoed through the glen.

"Kyle Makepeace," Kyle whispered.

"Yet you have been making war on Me most of your life," the voice chided.

Kyle lifted his head from the earth just enough to study his clenched fists.

"*WHAT IS YOUR NAME?*" the Voice thundered again. Cowed, Kyle covered his head and whimpered, "Echota."

"Yes, Echota," the Voice repeated insistently.

No one knew of this secret name given to him by his father at the bedside of his dying twin. His weeping Pa had groped for Crowe's hand and unknowingly grasped Kyle's. "My son, go forth now and be Echota," he had intoned, naming the ancient center of the Cherokee nation that had been a town of refuge and protection, a place of peace where all enmities were laid aside.

Kyle knew his father intended this as a prayer sending his first-born to a place of peace beyond death. But unwittingly he had bestowed it on Kyle as a mission, a quest that would define his life in this world. Guilt and grief had wiped the memory of that charge from Kyle's mind until this moment.

Lips against the earth, Kyle repeated, "Echota." Understanding flooded through him, reconciling the demands of his shaman-hood with that of his priestly ordination. In Echota, every fugitive could find protection and could

196

remain safe until forgiveness was obtained from any and all enemies. He, Kyle, had been sheltered there even when he thought he had fled from God into alien lands.

Someone touched his clenched fingers and Kyle looked up.

Crowe smiled down at him. "Why did you flee, my brother?"

"Did I not steal your life and your birthright?"

"What happened was meant to be," Crowe said softly.

"Can you forgive me?"

"Yes, I can forgive you, my brother, but you must claim the life that is yours and live it, damn it!" Crowe hissed fiercely and shoved Kyle back into the Branch.

Roughly he dunked Kyle over and over until Kyle understood. "Uncle!" he cried, "Uncle, uncle!" Laughter boomed around him as he scrambled out of the stream, caught Crowe with a flying tackle, and rolled over and over with him in a joyous wrestling match that neither cared to win or lose.

Exhausted at last, Kyle must have fallen asleep in the gentle sunlight, his hand still curved to grasp his brother's. He wakened with a start. How long had he slept? Where was Wren? He loped quickly back toward the falls.

Now where was she? Would she return to him? Could she? Anxiously he scanned the swirling waters, dreading to spot her battered body tossing in the foamy currents. He called out again, his voice taut with fear. Something glittered at the far edge of the basin where the waters had swept up bracken and debris.

Balancing precariously on the slippery edge of the pool, Kyle picked his way toward the tiny object. He recognized it instantly - the diamond studded wedding/ engagement band he had given Wren. Even as his hand closed around the precious object, he cried out her name in hopeless grief. The breeze swept his cry toward the falls and above the roar of white water, he seemed to hear an answer.

Looking up, Kyle saw Wren step out from behind the silver curtain of water several feet above the pool and climb swiftly down to him.

When Wren had first heard Kyle calling her, she had glanced up and discovered an exit from the grotto a few feet above her head. Clambering up the rocks with relief that she did not have to risk the pounding force of the falls again, Wren had slipped out from behind the roaring water. Kyle was still kneeling on the bank, anxiously scanning the foaming water. Only some of the worry left his face as he pulled Wren into his arms. She was so remote, so stiff in his embrace.

Picking up her boots, they found a place in the sun where their wet clothes could drip-dry as they talked. Uncertainty, anxiety, and doubt constrained them. The temptation to say nothing was strong but the very air about them protested such an escape. There was no returning to the cowardice they had brought with them to the Spring.

"This place may be called The Spring but it could also be named the Valley of Truth," Wren began softly, a grimace twitching her lips. "I've seen myself today... and, Kyle, believe me, when over thirty years of masks are ripped away, what is left is not pretty!"

Kyle regarded Wren intently. He said nothing but his eyes were eloquent with comprehension. He touched her hand encouragingly. Wren flinched and tried to withdraw her hand but Kyle grasped it more firmly. No matter how difficult, they must risk telling everything and leave nothing unspoken between them. Wren understood and gave up trying to reclaim her hand.

"So, can you tell me what happened behind the Falls?" Kyle asked.

Wren shook her head, droplets flying from her dark hair, just beginning to curl as it dried.

"Please, Wren!" Kyle urged, "Don't shut me out now! And

... don't shut yourself in."

"Why not?" Wren murmured, half to herself. "What does it matter to you?"

"Wren, I care. I love you!"

"Do you?" Wren flung out bitterly as she swiped at the water trickling down into her eyes.

I'm your husband, Wren!"

"Are you?"

Sudden understanding inundated Kyle like a smothering wave and he groaned. The ring cutting his palm had not been forcibly torn off Wren's finger by the waters. It had been deliberately thrown away. God damn it! Was there no end to the pain, the misunderstanding, the ... the refusals to deal with the truth? Wren shivered as water trickled down her back. Kyle still gripped her hand and oddly enough, she was glad for this physical connection.

"Well, what's to lose," Wren finally muttered, and turned to face Kyle squarely. "What happened behind the falls?" She paused. "At first, I didn't really care if I lived or died when I decided to dive into those waters. But when I felt I might actually drown, I fought until I finally surfaced. That first breath felt like heaven, a new life. Perhaps it is," she mused, a wry but sad expression settling on her mobile features.

Kyle resisted the urge to wrap her in his arms. Better not risk Wren clamming up on him again, as she had so often in the past.

"Behind the falls there is a shallow cave, a kind of grotto where... where an old black snake hangs out," Wren continued softly.

Kyle's eyes sharpened with concern, remembering how phobic Wren was about snakes.

"The snake was as big around as my calf!" she explained with a shudder. "When it slid across my foot, I just about threw myself back under the falls. But I couldn't move! Just like in my dreams ... but strangely, I didn't go mad with terror. Instead the snake seemed to draw the fear right out of me as it rippled over my foot. It went up on the altar..."

Kyle's dark eyebrows registered surprise. "Altar?"

"A stone in the middle of the cave that looks just like an altar," Wren explained. "The snake coiled up there and was still. As I stared, so fascinated and frightened I couldn't move, everything in me sort of grew still, oddly tranquil. I - I understood a lot in a few minutes."

Wren licked her lips. "Kyle, you know now who and what I am. If you want to leave our marriage... if it is a marriage... well, what can I say? But I'm afraid if you just walk out, leave like... like my mother did, I couldn't take that so," Wren drew a deep breath, "I've decided I'll opt out first and spare us both." She showed him the bare finger on her left hand.

Kyle made a move to speak but Wren's impatient gesture stopped him. "It's not fair to either of us to stay together now. I'm not the same woman you married or who walked into The Cove with you, Kyle. I feel like I've been ripped apart. God knows what I'll look like if and when I ever get put together again!" Wren concluded with a sound that was half-laugh, half-sob.

Kyle grimaced. "I wonder what you'll see in *me* now? Will you want a husband who has cried 'uncle'?"

"What?"

"I gave up, Wren. I can't run any longer, can't fight any more..."

"You? I've surrendered too, Kyle. I can't hate any more... myself or anyone else." (No, not even you, Kyle.) Wren added silently to herself.

She gnawed her knuckles and then looked up at the sun-browned man with the disheveled silvery hair. He looked so vulnerable and hurt. Wren touched his forehead shyly, "You've lost your headband, Kyle," she noted irrelevantly.

200

"Would that were all that was lost!" Kyle responded bitterly. The hurt and confusion in his dark eyes unexpectedly moved Wren. Suddenly she wondered how she could live without him. "Kyle, would you help me? Help me sort this out before... before you go." She shifted on the rocky bank, plucking at the mix of grass and wildflowers sprouting from the damp ground.

Kyle was so moved by Wren's unexpected plea, he didn't focus on the disturbing implications of the last phrase.

"Only if you will help me, Wren," he responded in a husky whisper that startled Wren out of her self-absorption.

She glanced up at Kyle. He was tugging at his nose, his brown cheeks stained even darker with shame. Slowly, painfully Kyle recounted his recent "baptism" and the exposure of his selfish cowardice, the acceptance of which had led to the recovery of his secret name. Wren listened deeply, wonderingly, to the multiple confessions of this man she thought she had known so well.

Finally, Kyle fell silent, feeling emptied, washed out, but also light, clean.

"Echota," Wren whispered. "Place of refuge ... oh, yes. Kyle, think what it means! Your life and Crowe's are still intertwined and you must live this call that claimed you long before you met me.

"You still share a name ... and a destiny with Crowe," Wren paused and bit her lip, "but that doesn't seem to leave any place for me!"

Kyle jerked. Wren's deduction startled him. She was seeing issues far more starkly than he. "What a damned fool I've been," he muttered. He turned toward Wren, stricken by the anguish written across her face. Ever since Crowe's death, he had felt only half-alive. Marriage to Wren had assuaged some of that ache, restored some sense of being a whole person. Now....? Kyle stared forlornly at this woman at his side, whom he had grievously deceived.

201

Hesitantly he touched Wren's face, brushing the auburn curls back off her cheek. When she didn't turn away, Kyle dared to ask. "For what I have done to you, Wren, can you forgive me? You've been changed and so have I, you know."

Wren nodded, touched by the tension and anxiety in Kyle's dark eyes. She put out her hand and gripped Kyle's arm imploringly. "Oh, I can forgive you, Kyle. But can there be a place for me in Echota's life, a place of refuge for a child of incest?"

"Do you still want to be with me ... after all this?" The ring burned in Kyle's palm.

Wren stared silently at the rushing branch water. Simultaneously, they realized that the entire valley was listening to Kyle's confession; to Wren's distress. All was being heard, absorbed, and accepted with a compassion as deep, as profound, and more ancient than the rocks surrounding them.

Shaken, Wren spoke words that surprised her. "Kyle, there seems to be so little left of who we were, nothing of what we'd told one another... of who we once thought we were... but somehow I want to believe, to hope ... that even those deceptions, those betrayals, are not so terrible they can't be forgiven; that people like us can start over, begin anew, learn what love, what trust really is." Wren studied the swirling waters of Lovada Branch as if she were listening intently to voices inaudible to Kyle.

Slowly she glanced upward to where The Spring leapt freely from the rocks above the falls. "Oh, yes," she said with a sigh, "yes, we are forgiven if we will only accept it." Then Wren turned to Kyle, her blue-green eyes were filled with a joy and peace Kyle had never seen there.

"Do you," Wren breathed softly, risking everything, "do you still want me in your life?"

In answer, Kyle opened his hand and revealed the ring he had recovered at the Spring.

Wren's jaw dropped. "You found it?"

Kyle nodded mutely, asking only with his eyes if she would take it back. Wren hesitated. What would it be like, married to a shaman, a priest? But this was Kyle asking, a Kyle who had deceived her yet still wanted, needed, loved her. She held out her left hand and Kyle slipped the ring back on her finger.

"With this ring, I pledge my life to yours," he mouthed softly. Swiftly, Kyle slipped off his own wedding band and gave it to Wren. She held it gently, the shyness back in her face. Reaching for Kyle's left hand, she kissed the ring and then slid it onto his finger. Kyle opened his arms and drew Wren close to him. Gratefully, silently, they leaned together in the cleansing sunlight.

After a while, Kyle's hand slid down Wren's breast and something stirred in her center. She lifted her head to receive his kiss, gentle at first but then hungry, responding to her ardor. Need, pain, and hope fueled the growing passion of their embrace. Kyle pressed Wren's head against his chest and she drew in the warm, familiar scent of his body, felt the sweet support of his arms about her. She tangled her fingers in his still damp hair. Priest and shaman, she wanted this man, wanted him passionately. What did it matter that she had to share him with Crowe, with God?

Kyle's fingers traced circles around her small firm breasts visible through her wet shirt, and suddenly, it didn't matter. Wren shifted until she was pressed tightly against his warm, lean body. Kyle took in a sharp breath as her movement suddenly, urgently wakened his need. Almost savagely, he tugged her damp shirt off and shrugged out of his. Meanwhile Wren fumbled at his jeans, freeing his swollen member. He drew off her jeans in a swift motion.

Sunlight poured over their naked flesh and they were not ashamed. What stopped them was a sudden, blinding

203

awareness of the beauty of one another. They slowly stood up and stepped apart like dancers in a formal set. Kyle's eyes ran over Wren's slender body, supple and glowing as he had never seen her.

Likewise, Wren took in the dark, lithe flesh of her man with a gentle awe, aware as never before of the holiness of the act they were initiating. Their coming together on the bed of spongy grass was reverent, powerful and more satisfying than anything either of them had experienced.

Later, entwined comfortably in one another's arms, they listened to the birds call, the insects hum, the waters chuckle and gurgle. Sunlight caressed them warmly, this man and woman who had come closer to expressing the eternal delight of the Holy than they had ever dreamed possible.

Wren sighed, her breath tickling Kyle's chest. 'There was something more I understood in the cave," Wren began quietly. "Do you remember that passage from the Bible, Kyle, the one about 'It has been told you, my people, what is required of you'?"

Kyle completed it, "'Only to act justly, love tenderly and walk humbly with your God.' Yes, I remember that. At one time, I felt it was the whole of Scripture in a nutshell. I guess I still do."

"It's the secret of The Cove, Kyle!" Wren murmured, her voice blending with the sibilant leaves about them. "It's what they are living here day by day. Without a formal 'church', are they not the most reverent and loving people we have ever met?"

Kyle nodded thoughtfully, "They are so open, so genuine. They're all so connected but there's nothing clannish about them and they certainly aren't a cult. I've never experienced such a liberating place." Kyle smiled and fondled Wren's relaxed breasts which immediately responded, nipples distending.

Wren slapped playfully at his hand. "Stop that! We're talking about more than one kind of freedom here."

Kyle nodded seriously. "Wren, you are Keeper of the Spring now. Do you know what that means? How can we keep faith with what we're learning here in the Cove? Where do we go from here?"

"I was about to ask that of you, Kyle Echota," Wren admitted.

As they leaned together, their heads touching, the myriad
Voices of the valley blended into words they had heard before, words that today were an anointing; a mission.

"To whom I send you, you shall go; whatever I command you, you shall speak. Have no fear before them, because I am with you to deliver you, says the Lord.... See, I place my words in your mouth! This day I set you... to root up and to tear down, to destroy and to demolish, to build and to plant."

Wren and Kyle stared at one another in shocked amazement until Wren whispered in a shaken voice, "Is that our answer?"

CHAPTER NINETEEN

Reluctant to leave the valley of the Spring, Wren and Kyle nevertheless felt as if they were being pushed out by a benevolent but implacable Spirit. Dressed in their now dry clothing, they took one long, last look at the falls, gilded by late afternoon rays. It had assumed the opalescence of mother-of-pearl, serene in its steady fall. Kneeling, they cupped the cold water in their hands, quenching more than their physical thirst.

Wren sat back on her heels. "Kyle, I just remembered a fragment of a poem I learned in college. Perhaps you could even call it a prayer." Kyle took her hand as she began:

"Spirit of the fountain; Spirit of the garden,
Suffer us not to mock ourselves with falsehood-
Teach us to care and not to care.
Teach us to sit still, even among these rocks.
Our peace in His will.
And even among these rocks.
Sister, mother,
And spirit of the river, spirit of the sea.
Suffer (us) not to be separated
And let (our) cry come unto thee."

For a moment all was still as if even the water of the falls had stopped in mid-flow. A bird called clearly, urgently far above them and the spell was broken. They wordlessly brushed water on one another's forehead. "We go with God," Wren breathed, and when Kyle questioned her with his eyes, she added, "No, I don't know if we shall ever return."

Kyle headed for the cleft in the rock that marked the hidden access to the valley, leaving Wren behind for a few moments of private farewell. Blooming among the ferns that flourished by the falls, she spotted a cluster of wild orchids, their rose-streaked blossoms glistening in the spray. Carefully she plucked a stalk and wrapped its stem in moss before hurrying after Kyle.

Scooting out from beneath the hemlock, they recovered the knapsack Kyle had left behind but not the knife. "Perhaps the Spirit of the Spring took it," he commented to Wren, and abandoned his search.

"No weapons needed where there is no fear?" she suggested.

Emerging from the shadows of the glen, Kyle was confused when Wren struck off in a direction opposite from what he thought they should take. After pointing this out, he was rewarded with chuckle from his wife who simply said, "Trust me. There are many ways to and from the Spring. This one will take us back to The Cove most directly. I want to get there before sundown."

Kyle felt thoroughly lost as they plunged into a thickly wooded area after crossing the rocky bald. His usually keen woods sense failed him utterly as he followed Wren's diminutive figure down a well-used animal trail that brought them to a bubbling run.

"A feeder stream for Lovada Branch," Wren explained, with the surety of one who had grown up on this mountain. Kyle eyed her keenly. Somewhere, somehow in the past day, Wren had assimilated the memories of generations of Lovada women and seemed as at home in the woods as

Kyle himself.

Silently, carefully their steps slowed as they walked through the rich woodland, alive with birdsong and the rustle of growing things. All around them, verdant life bloomed as spring's promise responded to early summer's long days. Their spirits tranquil as never before, Wren and Kyle ambled through shadow and sunlight, content in the moment. The silken chant of Lovada Branch in the background lulled them into a state of wordless prayer and profound peace. Wren smiled as her eyes caressed wildflowers, leaves, even insects that flickered gold among the dim trees. Blinders had been removed and she reveled in a world of beauty she had never before perceived.

Even so, it was Kyle who first glimpsed a stealthy movement among the trees ahead. "'Ware, Wren," he whispered. A tumble of huge granite boulders shadowed the path and they paused. Only when a shaft of sunlight caught a floppy gray hat did they move forward. Reaching Mencie's side, they were surprised to see both of their backpacks leaning against the rocks.

Kyle frowned, "What's up here? We were planning to stay on with Zettie for a few more days. Wren and I both have a lot to tell her. And I need to see Jonah...."

Mencie shook her head emphatically.

"Mamaw doesn't want to see us?" Wren asked, a trace of past hurt and uncertainty tinging her voice.

Flapping her hands, Mencie broke in, "Course, she wants to see you again. But you must leave at once. Things are happenin' out there and you are needed."

"But I want to tell her what happened at the Spring," Wren protested.

"Oh, she already knows, child," Mencie responded shortly. "Don't worry your head about that."

"How ...?" Wren began but Mencie forestalled her. "Don't ask. You'll understand when your turn comes. Right now, it's important that you get back to Laurel Spring as quickly as you can. Porter's family needs you, for one."

"His family? Oh, I forgot he was married," Wren paused in shock. "Did Zettie say he had three kids, Kyle?"

"Something like that," he muttered, his mind leapfrogging as he pondered their relationship to Wren.

"And that's not all," Mencie went on. She turned to Kyle.

"As soon as you get to Laurel Spring, look up Gaither. He'll tell you what you need to know."

"Old Gaither?" Kyle echoed. "What has he to do with The Cove? He didn't even want to talk about it. Why should he want to see me now?"

"Things are changin'," Mencie said simply. "and there's no time to lose." Before Wren or Kyle could object further, she helped them shoulder their packs.

Beckoning imperiously, she said, "Follow me, if you please," and led them along a narrow path not visible before.

Kyle and Wren exchanged mutual shrugs and plunged after her. In an incredibly short time, they found themselves at the trestle bridge. The further end was shrouded in mist.

"You know the way from here," Mencie waved her hat toward the bridge.

"Wait!" Wren cried out, and when Mencie looked toward her, Wren placed the rosy orchid from the Spring into Mencie's hand. "Would you give that to Mamaw?" she pleaded.

The gray gnome nodded, her features softening as she cupped Wren's chin in a hand surprisingly soft and smooth. "You don't feel ready, child, but trust me, you are. You and Kyle have much to do yet before ....." Mencie paused, gripped by uncharacteristic emotion. "I'm sorry we can't go with you but there will be others... you will find them." Mencie caressed Wren's cheek and turned to Kyle. She lifted her hand in a formal gesture and laid it briefly on Kyle's shoulder. "Forget not who you are," she warned sternly.

Mencie stepped back into the deepening shadows around them. Kyle and Wren suddenly found themselves with unasked questions still trembling on their lips.

"Well," Kyle grunted.

Wren nodded, "So! Just like this, it is over?"

"Over?" Kyle echoed, "I've a sinking feeling, it may be just beginning."

He turned toward the bridge and then glanced back at Wren. "Coming?" he asked.

"Oh, no! Oh. NO!"

Peering down into the gorge at their feet. Kyle offered, "We could try going down this cliff and climbing back up the other side if you don't want to cross the trestle."

Sidling as close to the edge as she dared, Wren demurred, "It's a near vertical descent. One slip and we'd roll non-stop to the bottom."

Kyle grunted in agreement. "So then..."

"Must we?" Wren asked in a small voice.

Kyle shrugged.

After a further period of silent struggle, Wren stepped behind Kyle and grasped the straps on his pack.

"Forward!" she commanded in a faint attempt at humor.

As Kyle's boot hit the first cross ties, he remembered Locke's story about the men Mencie had recently driven from the borderlands. They had reached the middle of the trestle only to have to clamber down the crossbars because the rest had been swept away. Definitely this was not the moment to share this info with Wren. Besides, he had a theory about this particular bridge....

When Kyle judged they were about halfway across, he stopped and looked back over Wren's shoulder. Slowly Wren swiveled in place to follow his gaze. In the gathering mists, a gray figure seemed to lift a floppy hat. Yellow eyes gleamed briefly.

Suddenly Wren shivered and turned to bury her head in Kyle's pack. "Do you suppose she'll be here when, if...."

"Wren," Kyle responded thoughtfully, "I don't think it would do any good 'supposin' anything about one like her." He reached back to caress her hand and they continued across the wet trestle.

On the bank behind them, the Dean watched, his plumey tail waving gently. Then he picked up a paw, licked it carefully and began washing his face. All was tranquil in the Borderlands as evening settled in. He had watched for them once and he would await their return. He was used to waiting.

What are *your* thoughts, feelings, insights, questions?

One reader observed about *THE COVE:* "*What spoke deeply to my soul, is the way you included all forms of love into the core of the book. The love expressed in compassion, the love friends have for one another, the love of the land, the love known in sexuality, the love of wisdom and the love of the Creator. Love to me, is the hub of the wheel around which the plot revolves.*"

How do *you* see the above?

What resonated with you among the commingled currents of Native American teaching, mountain lore, radical Christianity, nature's gifts and beauty, and the wisdom learned from an ancient land?

And let us not forget the role of the Elders!

Can you see the truth of The Cove and even the possibilities for such enclaves, hidden in plain sight, to being forth a redeemed future?

Has *The Cove* drawn you in? Do you feel summoned to follow the spirituality of *your* heart; *your* soul?

Let us talk. Let us share... You can reach Paul and Karen, plus other readers at www.ravensbreadministries.com/blog Or via email: pkfredette@frontier.com

Paul and Karen Fredette
18065 NC 209 Hwy.
Hot Springs, NC 28743

PH: 828 622 3750

Made in the USA
Columbia, SC
24 August 2019